"You might have given me a chance to open your door for you."

Dusty rolled her eyes. "You have to be kidding. Does anyone do that anymore?"

"I do when I pick up a woman," Ty said, sounding indignant. "It's polite."

"I can open my own door."

"That isn't the point. Look, think of dating as a game with certain rituals involved. There are steps to go through in the relationship. Roles each sex plays."

Dusty groaned. "Why does it have to be so complicated? Why can't we just cut to the chase?"

Ty shook his head. "Sorry, but it doesn't work that way. Anticipation adds to the excitement. It's all part of the mating ritual. You just need to get into your role."

Dusty scoffed. "This role you're talking about. Tell me it doesn't mean I have to act helpless, because I'm never going to be one of *those* women."

"Lucky for you, there are men who actually like strong, independent women. But no man may be ready for *you*."

Was Ty ready for her?

Dear Harlequin Intrigue Reader,

This July, Intrigue brings you six sizzling summer reads. They're the perfect beach accessory.

* We have three fantastic miniseries for you. *Film at Eleven* continues THE LANDRY BROTHERS by Kelsey Roberts. Gayle Wilson is back with the PHOENIX BROTHERHOOD in *Take No Prisoners*. And B.J. Daniels finishes up her McCALLS' MONTANA series with *Shotgun Surrender*.

* Susan Peterson brings you *Hard Evidence*, the final installment in our LIPSTICK LTD. promotion featuring stealthy sleuths. And, of course, we have a spine-tingling ECLIPSE title. This month's is Patricia Rosemoor's *Ghost Horse*.

* Don't miss Dana Marton's sexy stand-alone title, *The Sheik's Safety*. When an American soldier is caught behind enemy lines, she'll fake amnesia to guard her safety, but there's no stopping the sheik determined on winning her heart.

Enjoy our stellar lineup this month and every month!

Sincerely,

Denise O'Sullivan
Senior Editor
Harlequin Intrigue

SHOTGUN SURRENDER

B.J. DANIELS

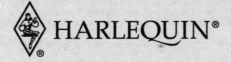

HARLEQUIN®

TORONTO • NEW YORK • LONDON
AMSTERDAM • PARIS • SYDNEY • HAMBURG
STOCKHOLM • ATHENS • TOKYO • MILAN • MADRID
PRAGUE • WARSAW • BUDAPEST • AUCKLAND

This one is for Kayley Mendenhall. A ray of sunshine
for everyone who has had the honor of knowing her.
Best wishes for a bright, fun and romantic future!

ISBN 0-373-22857-0

SHOTGUN SURRENDER

Copyright © 2005 by Barbara Heinlein

All rights reserved. Except for use in any review, the reproduction or
utilization of this work in whole or in part in any form by any electronic,
mechanical or other means, now known or hereafter invented, including
xerography, photocopying and recording, or in any information storage
or retrieval system, is forbidden without the written permission of the
publisher, Harlequin Enterprises Limited, 225 Duncan Mill Road,
Don Mills, Ontario, Canada M3B 3K9.

All characters in this book have no existence outside the imagination of
the author and have no relation whatsoever to anyone bearing the same
name or names. They are not even distantly inspired by any individual
known or unknown to the author, and all incidents are pure invention.

This edition published by arrangement with Harlequin Books S.A.

® and TM are trademarks of the publisher. Trademarks indicated with
® are registered in the United States Patent and Trademark Office, the
Canadian Trade Marks Office and in other countries.

www.eHarlequin.com

Printed in U.S.A.

ABOUT THE AUTHOR

A former award-winning journalist, B.J. Daniels had thirty-six short stories published before her first romantic suspense, *Odd Man Out,* came out in 1995. Her book *Premeditated Marriage* won *Romantic Times* Best Intrigue award for 2002 and she received a Career Achievement Award for Romantic Suspense. B.J. lives in Montana with her husband, Parker, three springer spaniels, Zoey, Scout and Spot, and a temperamental tomcat named Jeff. She is a member of Kiss of Death, the Bozeman Writer's Group and Romance Writers of America. When she isn't writing, she snowboards in the winters and camps, water-skis and plays tennis in the summers. To contact her, write: P.O. Box 183, Bozeman, MT 59771 or look for her online at www.bjdaniels.com.

Books by B.J. Daniels

CAST OF CHARACTERS

Dusty McCall—The youngest of the wild McCalls was ready for love. Only, she was looking for it in all the wrong places.

Ty Coltrane—The horse rancher knew something was wrong at the rodeo. He just didn't realize how wrong until he realized Dusty McCall was involved.

Boone Rasmussen—He had big plans for his future and a chip on his shoulder.

Letty Arnold—The news of her adoption had hit her hard. Now all she wanted was to find her birth mother. But she got more than she asked for.

Hal Branson—The private investigator had never believed in fate—until he met Letty Arnold.

Monte Edgewood—The roughstock producer thought he had everything until he got a chance to have a famous rodeo bull.

Sierra Edgewood—She had an old husband and a wandering eye and was built for trouble.

Lamar Nichols—The cowboy was supposed to be the brawn and not the brains of the operation, but even he could see what was going on.

Waylon Dobbs—The amicable rodeo veterinarian didn't believe in buying trouble. Unless there was something in it for him.

Devil's Tornado—He'd gone from a mediocre rodeo bull to a star overnight. But sometimes stars fall.

Prologue

The moment the pickup rolled to a stop, Clayton T. Brooks knew he should have put this off until morning. The night was darker than the inside of an outhouse, he was half-drunk and he couldn't see two feet in front of him.

Hell, maybe he was more than half-drunk since he was still seriously considering climbing the nearby fence and getting into a pasture with a bull that had almost killed its rider at a rodeo just a few days ago in Billings, Montana.

To make matters worse, Clayton knew he was too old for this sort of thing, not to mention physically shot from years of trying to ride the meanest, toughest bulls in the rodeo circuit.

But he'd never had the good sense to quit—until a bull messed him up so bad he was forced to. Just like now. He couldn't quit because he'd come this far and, damn, he needed to find out if he was losing his mind. Quietly he opened his pickup door and stepped out.

He'd coasted down the last hill with his headlights out, stopping far enough from Monte Edgewood's ranch house that he figured his truck wouldn't be heard when he left. There was no sign of life at the Edgewood Roughstock Company ranch at this hour of the night, but he wasn't taking any chances as he shut the pickup door as quietly as possible and headed for the pasture.

If he was right, he didn't want to get caught out here. The whole thing had been nagging him for days. Finally tonight, he'd left the bar when it closed, climbed into his pickup and headed out of Antelope Flats. It wasn't far to the ranch but he'd had to make a stop to get a six-pack of beer for the road.

Tonight he was going to prove himself wrong—or right—he thought as he awkwardly climbed the fence and eased down the other side. His eyes hadn't quite adjusted to the dark. Wisps of clouds drifted low across the black canvas stretched on the horizon. A few stars twinkled millions of miles away, and a slim silver crescent moon peeked in and out.

Clayton started across the small pasture, picking his way. Just over the rise, he froze as he made out the shape of the bull dead ahead.

Devil's Tornado was a Braford brindle-horned, one-ton bull—a breeder's Molotov cocktail of Brahma and Hereford. The mix didn't always turn out good bucking bulls, but it often did. The breed had ended more than a few cowboys' careers, his included.

He stared at the huge dark shape standing just yards

from him, remembering how the bull had damn near killed the rider at the Billings rodeo a few days before.

The problem was, Clayton thought he recognized the bull, not from Billings but from a town in Texas some years before. Thought he not only recognized the bull, but knew it intimately—the way only a bull rider gets to know a bull.

Unless he was losing his mind, he'd ridden this brindle down in Texas four years ago. It had been one of his last rides.

Only back then, the bull had been called Little Joe. And Little Joe had been less than an exciting ride. No tricks. Too nice to place deep on and make any prize money on.

The other bulls in the roughstock contractor's bag hadn't had any magic, either—the kiss of death for the roughstock contractor. Last Clayton had heard the roughstock outfit had gone belly-up.

Earlier tonight, he'd finally remembered the roughstock contractor's name. Rasmussen. The same last name as the young man who'd showed up a few weeks ago with a handful of bulls he was subcontracting out to Monte Edgewood.

If Clayton was right—and that was what he was here to find out—then Little Joe and Devil's Tornado were one and the same.

Except that the bull at the Billings rodeo had been a hot-tempered son-of-a-bucker who stood on its nose, hopped, skipped and spun like a top, quickly unseating the rider and nearly killing him. Nothing like the bull he'd ridden in Texas.

But Clayton was convinced this bull was Little Joe. Only with a definite personality change.

"Hey, boy," he called softly as he advanced. "Easy, boy."

The bull didn't move, seemed almost mesmerized as Clayton drew closer and closer until he could see the whites of the bull's enormous eyes.

"Hello, Little Joe." Clayton chuckled. Damned if he hadn't been right. Same notched ears, same crook in the tail, same brindle pattern. Little Joe was Devil's Tornado.

Clayton stared at the docile bull, trying to make sense of it. How could one bull be so different, not only from years ago but also from just days ago?

A sliver of worry burrowed under Clayton's skull. He definitely didn't like what he was thinking because if he was right...

He reached back to rub his neck only an instant before he realized he was no longer alone. He hadn't heard anyone approach from behind him, didn't even sense the presence until it was too late.

The first blow to the back of his head stunned him, dropping him to his knees next to the bull.

He flopped over onto his back and looked up. All he could make out was a dark shape standing over him and something long and black in a gloved hand.

Clayton didn't even get a chance to raise an arm to

ward off the second blow with the tire iron. The last thing he saw was the bull standing over him, the silver sickle moon reflected in the bull's dull eyes.

Chapter One

As the last cowboy picked himself up from the dirt, Dusty McCall climbed the side of the bucking horse chute.

"I want to ride," she said quietly to the elderly cowboy running this morning's bucking horse clinic.

Lou Whitman lifted a brow as he glanced down at the only horse left in the chute, a huge saddle bronc called The Undertaker, then back up at her.

He looked as if he was about to mention that she wasn't signed up for this clinic. Or that The Undertaker was his rankest bucking bronc. Or that her father, Asa McCall, or one of her four brothers, would have his behind if they found out he'd let her ride. Not when she was supposed to be helping "teach" this clinic—not ride.

But he must have seen something in her expression, heard it in her tone, that changed his mind.

He smiled and, nodding slowly, handed her the chest protector and helmet. "We got one more," he called to his crew.

She smiled her thanks at Lou as she took off her western straw hat and tossed it to one of the cowboys nearby. Slipping into the vest, she snugged down the helmet as Lou readied The Undertaker.

Swallowing any second thoughts, she lowered herself onto the saddle bronc in the chute.

None of the cowboys today had gone the required eight seconds for what was considered a legal rodeo ride.

She knew there was little chance of her being the first. Especially on the biggest, buckingest horse of the day.

She just hoped she could stay on long enough so that she wouldn't embarrass herself. Even better, that she wouldn't get killed!

"What's Dusty doing in there?" one of the cowboys along the corral fence wanted to know. "Dammit, she's just trying to show us up."

She ignored the men hanging on the fence as she readied herself. Bucking horses were big, often part draft horse and raised to buck. This one was huge, and she knew she was in for the ride of her life.

Not that she hadn't ridden saddle broncs before. She'd secretly taken Lou Whitman's clinic and ridden several saddle broncs just to show her brothers. Being the youngest McCall—and a girl on top of it—she'd spent her first twenty-one years proving she could do anything her brothers could—and oftentimes ended up in the dirt.

She doubted today would be any different. While she no longer felt the need to prove anything to herself and could care less about what her four older brothers thought, she had to do this.

And for all the wrong reasons.

"Easy, boy," she said as the horse banged around in the chute. She'd seen this horse throw some darned good cowboys in the past.

But she was going to ride him. One way or another. At least for a little while.

The horse shook his big head and snorted as he looked back at her. She could see her reflection in his eyes.

She leaned down to whisper in his ear, asking him to let her ride him, telling him how she needed this, explaining how much was at stake.

She could hear the cowboys, a low hum of voices on the corral fence. She didn't look, but imagined in her mind one in particular on the fence watching her, his dark eyes intrigued, his interest piqued.

Her body quaking with anticipation—and a healthy dose of apprehension—she gave Lou a nod to open the gate.

In that split second as the gate swung out, she felt the horse lunge and knew The Undertaker didn't give a damn that she was trying to impress some cowboy. This horse had his own agenda.

He shot straight up, jumped forward and came down bucking. He was big and strong and didn't feel like being ridden—maybe especially by her. Dust churned as he bucked and twisted, kicking and lunging as he set about unseating her.

But she stayed, remembering everything she'd been taught, everything she'd been teaching this morning along with Lou. Mostly, she stuck more out of stubborn determination than anything else.

She vaguely heard the sound of cheers and jeers over the pounding of hooves—and her heart.

When she heard the eight-second horn signaling she'd completed a legal rodeo ride, she couldn't believe it.

Too late, she remembered something her father always warned her about: pride goeth before the fall.

More than pleased with herself, she'd lost her focus for just an instant at the sound of the horn and glanced toward the fence, looking for that one cowboy. The horse made one huge lunging buck, and Dusty found herself airborne.

She hit the ground hard, the air knocked out of her. Dust rose around her in a cloud. Through it, she saw a couple cowboys jump down into the corral, one going after the horse, the other running to her.

Blinking through the dust, she tried to catch her breath as she looked up hoping to see the one cowboy she'd do just about anything to see leaning over her—Boone Rasmussen.

"You all right?" asked a deep male voice.

She focused on the man leaning over her and groaned. Ty Coltrane. The *last* cowboy she wanted to see right now.

"Fine," she managed to get out, unsure of that but not about to let him know if she wasn't.

She managed to sit up, looking around for Boone but didn't see him. The disappointment hurt more than the hard landing. Just before she'd decided to ride the horse, she'd seen Boone drive up. She'd just assumed he would join the others on the corral fence, that for once and for all, he would actually take notice of her.

"That was really something," Ty Coltrane commented sarcastically as he scowled down at her. Ty had been the bane of her existence since she'd been born. He raised Appaloosa horses on a ranch near her family's Sundown Ranch and every time she turned around, he seemed to be there, witnessing some of her most embarrassing moments—and causing more than a few.

And here he was again. It never failed.

She took off the helmet, her long blond braid falling free. Ty took the helmet and motioned to the cowboy on the fence, who tossed her western straw hat he'd been holding for her. It sailed through the air, landing short.

Ty picked it up from the dirt and slapped the dust off against his jeaned thigh. "Yep, that one could go down in the record book as one of the dumber things

I've seen you do, Slim." He handed her the hat, shaking his head at her.

As a kid, she'd been a beanpole, all elbows and knees, and she'd taken a lot of teasing about it. It had made her self-conscious. Even when she began to develop and actually had curves, she'd kept them hidden under her brothers' too large hand-me-down western shirts.

"Don't call me that," she snapped, glaring at him as she shoved the hat down on her blond head, tucking the single long braid up under it as she did.

He shook his head as if she mystified him. "What possessed you to ride The Undertaker? Have you lost all sense?"

The truth was, maybe she had. She didn't know what had gotten into her lately. Not that as a kid she hadn't always tried to be one of the boys and ride animals she shouldn't have. It came with being raised on an isolated ranch with four older brothers and their dumb friends.

That, and the fact that for most of her life, she'd just wanted to fit in, be one of the boys—not have them make fun of her, but treat her like one of their own.

All that had changed a few weeks ago when she'd first laid eyes on Boone Rasmussen. Suddenly, she didn't want to blend in anymore. She didn't want to be one of the boys. She felt things she'd only read about.

Now all she wanted was to be noticed by Boone Rasmussen.

And apparently there was no chance in hell of that ever happening.

"Here," Ty said extending a hand to help her up.

She ignored it as she got to her feet on her own and tried not to groan as she did. She'd be sore tomorrow if she could move at all. That *had* been a fool thing to do, but not for the reason Ty thought. She'd only done it to get Boone's attention. She couldn't believe she'd been so desperate, she thought as she took off the protective vest. Ty took it as well and handed both vest and helmet to one of the cowboys along the fence.

She hated feeling desperate.

Being that desperate made her mad and disgusted with herself. But the problem was, even being raised with four older brothers, she knew nothing about men. She hadn't dated much in high school, just a few dances or a movie. The boys she'd gone out with were like her, from God-fearing ranch families. None had been like Boone Rasmussen.

She realized that might be the problem. Boone was a *man*. And Boone had a reckless air about him that promised he was like no man *she'd* ever known.

"Nice ride," one of the cowboys told her as she limped out of the corral.

"Don't encourage her," Ty said beside her.

There was a time she would have been busting with pride. She'd ridden The Undertaker. She'd stayed on the eight seconds for the horn.

But today wasn't one of those days. The one cowboy she'd hoped to impress hadn't even seen her ride.

"You don't have to go telling my brothers about this," she warned Ty.

He grunted. "I have better things to do than go running to your brothers with stories about you," he said. "Anyway, the way you behave, it would be a full-time job."

She shot him a narrow-eyed look, then surreptitiously glanced around for Boone Rasmussen, spotting him over by the bull corrals talking to the big burly cowboy who worked with him, Lamar something or other.

Boone didn't even glance in her direction and obviously hadn't seen her ride or cared. Suddenly, she felt close to tears and was spitting mad at herself.

"You sure you're all right?" Ty asked as he reached to open her pickup door for her.

She could feel his gaze on her. "I told you I'm fine," she snapped, fighting tears. What was wrong with her? She normally would rather swallow tacks than cry in front of him or one of her brothers.

"You're sure you're up to driving back to the ranch by yourself?" he asked, only making her feel worse.

She fought a swell of emotion as she climbed into the pickup seat and started to close the door.

Ty stopped her by covering her hand on the door handle with his. "Okay, Slim, that was one hell of a ride. You stayed on longer than any of those cowboys. And you rode The Undertaker. Feel better?"

She looked at him, tears welling in her eyes. He thought she was mad at *him* because he'd chewed her out for riding today?

She half smiled at him, filled with a sudden stab of affection. Funny, but since Boone, she even felt differently about Ty.

Unlike Boone though, Ty had blue eyes like her own. There was no mystery about Ty. She'd known him her whole life. Boone on the other hand, had dark eyes, mysterious eyes, and everything about him felt…dangerous.

"You wouldn't understand even if I could explain it," she said.

Ty smiled ruefully and reached out to pluck a piece of straw from a stray strand of her blond hair. "Probably not, Slim, but maybe it's time you grew up before you break your fool neck." He let go of her hand and she slammed the pickup door. So much for the stab of affection she'd felt for him.

Grow up? Without looking at him, she started the truck and fought the urge to roll down her window and tell him what she thought. But when she glanced over, Ty had already walked away.

She sat for a moment in a stew of her own emotions. The worst part was, Ty was right. It was definitely time for her to grow up. Too bad she didn't have the first clue how to do that.

She shifted the pickup into gear. Boone Rasmussen was still talking to Lamar by the chutes. He didn't look up as she pulled away.

TY MENTALLY KICKED HIMSELF all the way to his truck. He'd only come by the rodeo grounds this morning to see if Clayton T. Brooks was around. The old bull rider hadn't shown up for work.

Everyone said Ty was a fool for hiring him. Even part-time. But Clayton was a good worker and Ty knew Clayton needed the money. Sometimes he showed up late, but he always showed for work. Until today.

"Any of you seen Clayton today?" he called to the handful of men on the corral fence. Several of the cowboys were trying to get Lou to let them ride again. Couldn't let some little gal like Dusty McCall show them up.

"Saw him at the bar *last night*," one of them called back. "He was three sheets to the wind and going on about some bull." The cowboy shook his head. "You know Clayton. Haven't seen him since, though." The rest shook their heads in agreement.

"Thanks." Ty *did* know Clayton. For most of his life, Clayton had ridden bulls. Now that he couldn't ride anymore, he "talked" bulls. Or talked "bull," as some said.

Still, Ty was worried about him. He decided to swing by Clayton's trailer on the opposite side of town before returning to the ranch.

Dusty McCall drove past as Ty climbed into his truck. He let out a sigh as he watched her leave. All he'd done was make her mad. But the fool girl could have gotten herself killed. What had been going on with her lately?

Not your business, Coltrane.

Didn't he know it.

In spite of himself, he smiled at the memory of her riding that saddle bronc. She was something, he thought with a shake of his head. Unfortunately, she saw him at best as the cowboy next door. At worst, as another older brother, as if she needed another one.

He shook off that train of thought like a dog shaking off water and considered what might have happened to Clayton as he started his pickup and drove into town.

Antelope Flats was a small western town with little more than a café, motel, gas station and general store. The main business was coal or coal-bed methane gas. Those who worked either in the open-pit coal mine or for the gas companies lived twenty-plus miles away in Sheridan, Wyoming, where there was a movie theater, pizza parlors, clothing stores and real grocery stores.

Between Antelope Flats and Sheridan there was nothing but sagebrush-studded hills and river bottom, and with deer, antelope, geese, ducks and a few wild turkeys along the way.

Antelope Flats had grown some with the discovery of coal-bed methane gas in the land around town. There was now a drive-in burger joint on the far edge of town, a minimall coming in and talk of a real grocery store.

Ty hoped to hell the town didn't change too much

in the coming years. This was home. He'd been born and raised just outside of here, and he didn't want the lifestyle to change because of progress. He knew he sounded like his father, rest his soul. But family ranches were a dying breed and Ty wanted to raise his children on the Coltrane Appaloosa Ranch just as he'd been raised.

Clayton T. Brooks had bought a piece of ground out past town and put a small travel trailer on it. The trailer had seen better days. So had the dated old pickup the bull rider drove. The truck wasn't out front, but Ty parked in front of the trailer and got out anyway.

The sun was high in a cloudless blue sky. He could smell the cottonwoods and the river and felt the early spring heat on his back as he knocked on the trailer.

No answer.

He tried the door.

It opened. "Clayton?" he called as he stepped into the cool darkness. The inside was neater than Ty had expected it would be. Clayton's bed at the back looked as if he'd made it before he left this morning. Or hadn't slept in it last night. No dishes in the sink. No sign that Clayton had been here.

As Ty left, he couldn't shake the bad feeling that had settled over him. Yesterday, Clayton had been all worked up over some bull ride he'd seen the weekend before at the Billings rodeo.

Ty hated to admit he hadn't been listening that closely. Clayton was often worked up about something and almost always it had to do with bulls or riders or rodeo.

Was it possible Clayton had taken off to Billings because of some damn bull?

TEXAS-BORN BOONE RASMUSSEN had been cursed from birth. It was the only thing that explained why he'd been broke and down on his luck all twenty-seven years.

He left the rodeo grounds and drove the twenty miles north of town turning onto the road to the Edgewood Roughstock Company ranch. The road wound back in a good five more miles, a narrow dirt track that dropped down a series of hills and over a creek before coming to a dead end at the ranch house.

Boone could forgive those first twenty-seven years if he had some promise that the next fifty were going to be better. He was certainly due for some luck. But he'd been disappointed a few too many times to put much stock in hope. Not that his latest scheme wasn't a damned good one.

He didn't see Monte's truck as he parked in the shade of the barn and glanced toward the rambling old two-story ranch house. A curtain moved on the lower floor. She'd seen him come back, was no doubt waiting for him.

He swore and tried to ignore the quickened beat of his heart or the stirring below his belt. At least he was smart enough not to get out of the truck. He glanced over at the bulls in a nearby pasture, worry gnawing at his insides, eating away at his confidence.

So far he'd done two things right—buying back a few of his father's rodeo bulls after the old man's death and hooking up with Monte Edgewood.

But Boone worried he would screw this up, just like he did everything else. If he hadn't already.

He heard someone beside the truck and feared for a moment she had come out of the house after him.

With a start, he turned to find Monte Edgewood standing at the side window. Monte had been frowning, but now smiled. "You goin' to just sit in your pickup all day?"

Boone tried to rid himself of the bitter taste in his mouth as he gave the older man what would pass for a smile and rolled down his window. Better Monte never know why Boone had been avoiding the house in his absence.

"You all right, son?" Monte asked.

Monte Edgewood had called him son since the first time they'd met behind falling-down rodeo stands in some hot, two-bit town in Texas. Boone had been all of twelve at the time. His father was kicking the crap out of him when Monte Edgewood had come along, hauled G. O. Rasmussen off and probably saved Boone's life.

In that way, Boone supposed he owed him. But what Boone hadn't been able to stand was the pity he'd seen in Monte's eyes. He'd scrambled up from the dirt and run at Monte, fists flying, humiliation and anger like rocket fuel in his blood.

A huge man, Monte Edgewood had grabbed him in a bear hug, pinning his skinny flailing arms as Boone struggled furiously to hurt someone the way he'd been hurt. But Monte was having none of it.

Boone fought him, but Monte refused to let go. Finally spent, Boone collapsed in the older man's arms. Monte released him, reached down and picked up Boone's straw hat from the dust and handed it to him.

Then, without a word, Monte just turned and walked away. Later Boone heard that someone jumped his old man in an alley after the rodeo and kicked the living hell out of him. Boone had always suspected it had been Monte, the most nonviolent man he'd ever met.

Unfortunately, Boone had never been able to forget the pity he'd seen in Monte's eyes that day. Nor the sour taste of humiliation. He associated both with the man because of it. Kindness was sometimes the worse cut of all, he thought.

Monte stepped back as Boone opened his door and got out. Middle age hadn't diminished Monte's size, nor had it slowed him down. His hair under his western hat was thick and peppered with gray, his face rugged. At fifty, Monte Edgewood was in his prime.

He owned some decent enough roughstock and quite a lot of land. Monte Edgewood seemed to have everything he needed or wanted. Unlike Boone.

But what made Monte unique was that he was without doubt the most trusting man Boone had ever met.

And that, he thought with little remorse, would be Monte's downfall. And Boone's good fortune.

"How's Devil's Tornado today?" Boone asked as they walked toward the ranch house where Monte had given him a room. He saw the curtain move and caught a glimpse of dyed blond hair.

"Son, you've got yourself one hell of a bull there," Monte said, laying a hand on Boone's shoulder as they mounted the steps.

Didn't Boone know it.

Monte opened the screen and they stepped into the cool dimness of the house and the heady scent of perfume.

"Is that you, Monte?" Sierra Edgewood called an instant before she appeared in the kitchen doorway, a sexy silhouette as she leaned lazily against the jamb and smiled at them. "Hey, Boone."

He nodded in greeting. Sierra wore a cropped top and painted-on jeans, a healthy width of firm sun-bronzed skin exposed between the two. She was pinup-girl pretty and was at least twenty years younger than her husband.

"It will be interesting to see how he does in Bozeman," Monte continued as he slipped past his wife, planting a kiss on her neck as he headed for the fridge. He didn't seem to notice that Sierra was still blocking the kitchen doorway as he took out two cold beers and offered one to Boone.

After a moment, Sierra moved to let Boone pass, an amused smile on her face.

"He's already getting a reputation among the cowboys," Monte said heading for the kitchen table with the beers as if he hadn't noticed what Sierra was up to. He never seemed to. "Everyone's looking for a high-scoring bull and one hell of a ride."

Boone sat down at the table across from Monte and took the cold beer, trying to ignore Sierra.

"Are you talking about that stupid bull again?" she asked as she opened the fridge and took out a cola. She popped the cap off noisily, pushing out her lower lip and giving Boone the big eyes as she sat down across from him.

A moment later, he felt her bare toes run from the top of his boot up the inside seam of his jeans. He shifted, turning to stretch his legs out far enough away that she couldn't touch him as he took a deep drink of his beer. He heard Sierra sigh, a chuckle just under the surface.

He knew he didn't fool her. She seemed only too aware of what she did to him. His blood running hot, he focused on the pasture out the window and Devil's Tornado, his ticket out, telling himself all the Sierra Edgewoods in the world couldn't tempt him. There was no greater lure than success. And failure, especially this time, would land him in jail—if not six feet under.

Devil's Tornado could be the beginning of the life

Boone had always dreamed of—as long as he didn't blow it, he thought, stealing a sidelong glance at Sierra.

"Everyone's talking about your bull, son," Monte said with pride in his voice but also a note of sadness.

Boone looked over at him, saw the furrowed thick brows and hoped Monte was worried about Devil's Tornado—not Boone and his wife.

There was a fine line between a bull a rider could score on and one who killed cowboys. And Devil's Tornado had stomped all over that line at the Billings rodeo. Boone couldn't let that happen again.

Sierra tucked a lock of dyed-blond hair behind her ear and slipped her lips over the top of the cola bottle, taking a long cool drink before saying, "So what's the problem?"

Monte smiled at her the way a father might at his young child. "There's no problem."

But that wasn't what his gaze said when he settled it back on Boone.

"The bull can be *too* dangerous," Boone told her, making a point he knew Monte had been trying to make. "It's one thing to throw cowboys—even hurt a few. But if he can't be ridden and he starts killing cowboys, then I'd have to take him off the circuit." He shrugged as if that would be all right. "He'd be worth some in stud fees or an artificial insemination breeding program at this point. But nothing like he would be if, say, he was selected for the National Finals Rodeo in Las Vegas. It would be too bad to put him out to pasture now, though. We'd never know just how far he might have gone."

A shot at having a bull in the National Finals in Las Vegas meant fifty thousand easy, not to mention the bulls he would sire. Everyone would want a piece of that bull. A man could make a living for years off one star bull.

That's why every roughstock producer's dream was a bull like that. Even Monte Edgewood, Boone was beginning to suspect. But only the top-scoring bulls in the country made it. Devil's Tornado seemed to have what it took to get there.

"I wouldn't pull him yet," Monte said quickly, making Boone smile to himself. Monte had needed a bull like Devil's Tornado.

And Boone needed Monte's status as one of the reputable roughstock producers.

After more rodeos, more incredible performances, everyone on the circuit would be talking about Devil's Tornado. That's when Boone would pull him and start collecting breeding fees, because it wouldn't matter if the bull could make the National Finals. Boone could never allow Devil's Tornado to go to Vegas.

But in the meantime, Devil's Tornado would continue to cause talk, his value going up with each rodeo.

If the bull didn't kill his next rider.

Or flip out again like he did in Billings, causing so much trouble in the chute that he'd almost been pulled.

Devil's Tornado was just the first. If this actually

worked, Boone could make other bulls stars. He could write his own ticket after that.

But he could also crash and burn if he got too greedy, if his bulls were so dangerous that people got suspicious.

Monte finished his beer and stared at the empty bottle. "I don't have to tell you what a competitive business this is. You've got to have good bulls that a cowboy can make pay for them. But at the same time you don't want PETA coming down on you or those Buck the Rodeo people."

Boone had seen the ads—Buck the Rodeo: Nobody likes an eight-second ride!

Monte looked over at him. "When I got into this business, I promised myself that the integrity of the rodeo and the safety of the competitors would always come first. You know what I'm saying, son?"

Boone knew *exactly* what he was saying. He looked out the window to where Devil's Tornado stood in his own small pasture flicking his tail, the sun gleaming off his horns, then back across the table at Sierra Edgewood. Boone had better be careful. More careful than he had been.

Chapter Two

Sundown Ranch

Asa McCall heard the creak of a floorboard. He turned to find his wife standing in the tack room doorway. His wife. After so many years of being apart, the words sounded strange.

"What do you think you're doing?" Shelby asked, worry making her eyes dark.

"I'm saddling my horse," he said as he hefted the saddle and walked over to the horse. The motion took more effort than it had even a few weeks ago. He hoped she hadn't noticed, but then Shelby noticed everything.

"I can see that," she said, irritation in her tone as she followed him.

Shelby Ward McCall was as beautiful as the day he'd met her forty-four years ago. She was tall and slim, blond and blue-eyed, but her looks had never impressed him as much as her strength. They both knew she'd always been stronger than he was, even though he was twice her size—a large, powerfully built man with more weaknesses than she would ever have.

He wondered now if that—and the fact that they both knew it—had been one of the reasons she'd left him thirty years ago. He knew damn well it was the reason she had come back.

"I'm going for a ride," he said, his back to her as he cinched the saddle in place, already winded by the physical exertion. He was instantly angry at himself. He despised frailty, especially in himself. He'd always been strong, virile, his word the last. He'd never been physically weak before, and he found that nearly impossible to live with.

"Asa—" Her voice broke.

"Don't," he said shaking his head slightly, but even that small movement made him nauseous. "I need to do this." He hated the emotion in his voice. Hated that she'd come back to see him like this.

Shelby looked away. She knew he wouldn't want her to see how pathetic he'd become. He wished he could hide not only his weakness but his feelings from her, but that was impossible. Shelby knew him with an intimacy that had scared him. As if she could see into his black soul and still find hope for him. Still love him.

"I could come with you," she said without looking at him.

"No, thank you," he added, relieved when she didn't argue the point. He didn't need a lecture on how dangerous it was for him to go riding alone. He had hoped to die in the saddle. He should be so lucky.

He swung awkwardly up onto the horse, giving her a final look, realizing how final it would soon be. He never tired of looking at her and just the thought of how many years he'd pushed her away from him brought tears to his eyes. He'd become a doddering sentimental old fool on top of everything else. He spurred the horse and rode past her and out of the barn, despising himself.

At the gate, something stronger than even his will forced him to turn and look back. She was slumped against the barn wall, shoulders hunched, head down.

He cursed her for coming back after all the years they'd lived apart and spurred his horse. Cursed himself. As he rode up through the foothills of the ranch his father had started from nothing more than a scrawny herd of longhorn cattle over a hundred years ago, he was stricken with a pain far greater than any he had yet endured.

His agony was about to end, but it had only begun for his family. He would have to tell them everything.

He tried not to think about what his sons and daughter would say when he told them that years ago, he'd sold his soul to the devil, and the devil was now at his door, ready to collect in more ways than one.

J.T., his oldest, would be furious; Rourke would be disappointed; Cash would try to help, as always; and Brandon possibly would be relieved to find that his father was human after all. Dusty, his precious daughter, the heart of his heart… Asa closed his eyes at the thought of what it would do to her.

He would have to tell them soon. He might be weak in body and often spirit, but he refused to be a coward. He couldn't let them find out everything after he was gone. Not when what he'd done would put an end to the Sundown Ranch as they all knew it.

Sheridan, Wyoming, rodeo

IT WAS FULL DARK and the rodeo was almost over by the time Ty Coltrane made his way along the packed grandstands.

He'd timed it so he could catch the bull riding. No one he'd talked to had seen Clayton, nor had there been any word. But Ty knew that if Clayton was anywhere within a hundred-mile radius, he wouldn't miss tonight's rodeo.

Glancing around before the event started, though, he didn't see the old bull rider. He did, however, see Dusty McCall and her friend, Leticia Arnold, sitting close to the arena fence.

Dusty didn't look the worse for wear after her bucking bronc performance earlier today. He shook his head at the memory, telling himself he was tired of playing nursemaid to her. She wasn't his responsibility. He couldn't keep picking her up from the dirt. What if one day he wasn't around to save her skinny behind?

"Now in chute three, we've got a bull that's been

making a stir across the country," the announcer bellowed over the sound system. "He's called Devil's Tornado and for a darned good reason. Only a few cowboys have been able to ride him, and those who have scored big. Tonight, Huck Kramer out of Cheyenne is going to give it a try."

Ty felt a start. Devil's Tornado. *That* was the bull that Clayton had been so worked up over. Ty was sure of it. He angled his way through the crowd so he could see the bull chutes as he tried to recall what exactly Clayton had said about the bull.

Devil's Tornado banged around inside the chute as Huck lowered himself onto it to the jangle of the cowbell attached to his rosin-coated bull rope. The cowbell acted as a weight, allowing the rope to safely fall off the bull when the ride was over. Riders used rosin, a sticky substance that increased the grip on their ropes, to make sure they were secured to the bull in hopes of hanging on for the eight-second horn.

Huck wrapped the end of the bull rope tightly around his gloved hand, securing himself to the one-ton bull. Around the bull was a bucking rigging, a padded strap that was designed to make the bull buck.

A hush fell over the crowd as the bull snorted and kicked at the chute, growing more agitated. Huck gave a nod of his head and the chute door flew open with a bang and Devil's Tornado came bursting out in a blur of movement.

Instantly, Ty knew this was not just any bull.

So did the crowd. A breath-stealing silence fell over the rodeo arena as Devil's Tornado slammed into the fence, then spun in a tight bucking cyclone of dust and hooves.

Devil's Tornado pounded the earth in bucking lunges, hammering Huck with each jarring slam. Ty watched, his heart in his throat as the two-thousand pound bull's frantic movements intensified in a blur of rider and bull.

The crowd found its voice as the eight-second horn sounded and bullfighters dressed like clowns rushed out.

With his hand still tethered to the monstrous bull, Huck's body suddenly began to flop from side to side, as lifeless as a dummy's, as Devil's Tornado continued bucking.

The bullfighters ran to the bull and rider, one working frantically to free the bucking rigging from around the bull and the other to free Huck's arm from the thickly braided rope that bound bull and rider.

Devil's Tornado whirled, tossing Huck from side to side, charging at the bullfighters who tried desperately to free the rider. One freed the rigging strap designed to make the bull buck. It fell to the dirt, but Huck's bull rope wouldn't come loose. The cowbell jangled at the end of the rope as Huck flopped on the bull's broad back as the bull continued to buck and spin in a nauseating whir of motion.

Other cowboys had jumped into the arena, all fighting to free Huck. It seemed to go on forever, although it had only been a matter of seconds before one of the bullfighters pulled a knife, severing Huck from Devil's Tornado.

Huck's lifeless body rose one last time into the air over the bull, suspended like a bag of rags for a heart-stopping moment before it crumpled to the dirt.

The crowd swelled to its feet in a collective gasp of horror as the rider lay motionless.

Devil's Tornado made a run for the body. A bullfighter leapt in front of the charging bull and was almost gored. He managed to distract the bull away from Huck, but only for a few moments.

The bull started to charge one of the pickup riders on horseback, but stumbled and fell. He staggered to his feet in a clear rage, tongue out, eyes rolling.

Cowboys jumped off the fence to run to where Huck lay crumpled in the dirt. A leg moved. Then an arm. Miraculously, Huck Kramer sat up, signally he was all right.

A roar of applause erupted from the grandstands.

"That was some ride," the announcer said over the loudspeaker. "Let's give that cowboy another round of applause."

Ty sagged a little with relief. He hated to see cowboys get hurt, let alone killed. Huck had been lucky.

Ty's gaze returned to Devil's Tornado. The bull ran wild-eyed around the other end of the arena, charging at anything that moved, sending cowboys clambering up the fence. Ty had seen this many times during bull rides at rodeos.

Devil's Tornado was big and strong, fast out of the chute and one hell of a bucker, but those were attributes, nothing that would have gotten Clayton worked up.

"Whew," the announcer boomed. "Folks, you aren't going to believe this. The judges have given Huck a whopping ninety-two!"

The crowd cheered as Huck was helped out of the arena. He seemed to be limping but, other than that, okay.

Had Clayton just been impressed by Devil's Tornado? No. Ty distinctly remembered that Clayton had been upset, seemingly worried about something he'd seen at the Billings rodeo involving Devil's Tornado. But what?

The pickup riders finally cornered the bull, one getting a rope around the head and a horn and worked him toward the exit chute. Devil's Tornado pawed the earth, shaking his head, fighting them.

Ty worked his way in the direction of the exit chute, hoping to get a closer look. As Devil's Tornado was being herded out, he seemed disoriented and confused, shying away from anything that moved.

Usually, by the time a bull got to the exit chute, he recognized that it was over and became more docile. Not Devil's Tornado. He still seemed worked up, maybe a little high-strung, stopping when he saw the waiting semitrailer, looking scared and unsure. Still, not that unusual for a bull that had just scored that high a ride.

Ty wouldn't have thought anything more about the bull if he hadn't seen Boone Rasmussen rush up to the exit chute and reach through the fence to touch the still aggravated Devil's Tornado. What the hell? Ty couldn't see what Boone had done, but whatever it was made the bull stumble back, almost falling again. Rasmussen reached again for the bull, then quickly withdrew his hand, thrusting it deep into his jacket pocket.

How strange, Ty thought. Devil's Tornado was frothing at the mouth, his head lolling. Ty saw the bull's eyes. Wide and filled with…panic? Devil's Tornado looked around crazily as if unable to focus.

Ty tried to remember where he'd seen that look on a bull before and it finally came to him. It had been years ago in a Mexican bull ring. He was just a kid at the time, but he would never forget that crazed look in the bull's eyes.

Is this what Clayton had witnessed? Is this what had him so upset? Had Clayton suspected something was wrong with Devil's Tornado, just as Ty did? But what would Clayton have done about it?

Ty wasn't even sure what he'd just witnessed. All he knew was: something was wrong with that bull. And Boone Rasmussen was at the heart of it.

"Did you see that?" Letty asked, sitting next to her friend.

Dusty stared through the arena fence toward the chutes and Boone Rasmussen, not sure what she'd seen or what she was feeling right now. "See what?"

Letty let out an impatient sigh. "Don't tell me you missed the entire bull ride because you were gawking at Boone Rasmussen."

Dusty looked over at her friend, surprised how off balance she felt. She let out a little chuckle and pretended she wasn't shaking inside. "Some ride, huh."

But it wasn't the ride that had her hugging herself to ward off a chill on such a warm spring night. She wasn't sure what she'd seen. Letty, like everyone else, had been watching Huck Kramer once the bull had gone into the chutes.

Dusty had been watching Boone. That's why she'd seen the expression on his face when he reached through the fence and hit Devil's Tornado with something. Not a cattle prod but something else. The bull had been in her line of sight, so she couldn't be sure what it had been.

Boone Rasmussen's expression had been so…cold. It all happened so fast—the movement, Boone's expression. But there was that moment when she wondered if she'd made a mistake when it came to him. Maybe he wasn't what she was looking for at all.

Ty moved along the corrals to the exit chute where Devil's Tornado now stood, head down, unmoving.

Rasmussen stood next to the fence as if watching the bull, waiting. Waiting for what?

A chill ran the length of his spine as Ty stared at Devil's Tornado. This had to be what Clayton had seen. The look in that bull's eyes and Rasmussen acting just as strangely as the bull.

"Where do you think you're going?" Lamar Nichols stepped in front of him, blocking his view of the bull and Rasmussen.

Ty looked past the big burly cowboy to where Rasmussen prodded the bull and Devil's Tornado stumbled up into the trailer. Rasmussen closed the door behind it with a loud clank.

A shudder went through Ty at the sound. "That's some bull you got there."

"He don't like people." Lamar stepped in front of him, blocking his view again. "Unless you're authorized to be back here, I suggest you go back into the stands with the rest of the audience."

Ty looked past Lamar and saw Rasmussen over by the semitrailer. "Sure," Ty said to the barrel-chested cowboy blocking his way. No chance of getting a closer look now.

He knew if he tried, Lamar would call security or take a swing at him. Ty didn't want to create that much attention.

As Ty headed back toward the grandstand, he searched the crowd for Clayton T. Brooks with growing concern. Now more than ever, he wanted to talk to the old bull rider about Devil's Tornado and what had happened at the Billings rodeo that had riled Clayton.

But Ty didn't see him in the crowd or along the fence with the other cowboys. Where was Clayton anyway? He never missed a rodeo this close to home.

"THANKS FOR HANGING AROUND with me," Dusty Mc-Call said as she and her best friend, Leticia Arnold, walked past the empty dark grandstands after the rodeo.

The crowd had gone home. But Dusty had waited around, coming up with lame excuses to keep her friend there because she hadn't wanted to stay alone—and yet she'd been determined not to leave until she saw Boone.

But she never got the chance. Either he'd left or she just hadn't seen him among the other cowboys loading stock.

"I'm pathetic," Dusty said with another groan.

Letty laughed. "No, you're not."

"It's just…" She waved her hand through the air unable to explain all the feelings that had bombarded her from the first time she'd laid eyes on Boone a few weeks before. He was the first man who'd ever made her feel like this, and it confused and frustrated her to no end.

"Are you limping?" Letty asked, frowning at her.

"It's nothing. Just a little accident I had earlier today," Dusty said, not wanting to admit she'd ridden a saddle bronc just to impress Boone and he hadn't even seen her ride. She hated to admit even to herself how stupidly she'd been behaving.

"Are you sure Boone's worth it?" Letty asked.

Right at that moment, no.

"He just doesn't seem like your type," her friend said.

Dusty had heard all of this before. She didn't want to hear it tonight. Especially since Letty was right. She didn't understand this attraction to Boone any more than Letty did. "He's just so different from any man I've ever met," she tried to explain.

"That could be a clue right there."

Dusty gave her friend a pointed look. "You have to admit he *is* good-looking."

"In a dark and dangerous kind of way, I suppose," Letty agreed.

Dark and dangerous. Wasn't that the great attraction, Dusty thought, glancing back over her shoulder toward the rodeo arena. She felt a small shiver as she remembered the look on his face when he'd reached through the fence toward the bull. She frowned, realizing that she'd seen something drop to the ground as Boone pulled back his hand. Something that had caught the light. Something shiny. Like metal. Right after that Monte had picked whatever it was up from the ground and pocketed it.

"You're sure he told you to meet him after the rodeo?" Letty asked, not for the first time.

Dusty had told a small fib in her zeal to see Boone

tonight. On her way back from getting a soda, she'd seen Boone, heard him say, "Meet me after the rodeo." No way was he talking to her. He didn't know she existed. But when she'd related the story to Letty, she'd let on that she thought Boone had been talking to her.

"Maybe I got it wrong," Dusty said now.

Maybe she'd gotten everything wrong. But that didn't explain these feelings she'd been having lately. If she hadn't been raised in a male-dominated family out in the boonies and hadn't spent most of her twenty-one years up before the sun mending fence, riding range and slopping out horse stalls, she might know what to do with these alien yearnings. More to the point, what to do about these conflicting emotions when it came to Boone Rasmussen.

Instead, she felt inept, something she wasn't used to. She'd always been pretty good at everything she tried. She could ride and rope and round up cattle with the best of them, and she'd been helping run the ranch for the past few years since her father's heart attack.

But even with four older brothers, she knew squat about men. Well, one man in particular, Boone Rasmussen. And after tonight, she felt even more confused. She wasn't even sure that once she got his attention, talked to him, that she would even like him. Worse, she couldn't get that one instant, when he'd reached through the fence, out of her mind. What had fallen on the ground?

"Dusty?" Letty was a few yards ahead, looking back at her.

Dusty hadn't realized that she'd stopped walking.

But then again, she was a McCall. She'd been raised to go after what she wanted. And anyway, she couldn't wait around for Boone to make the first move. Heck, she could be ninety before that happened. She was also curious about what Boone had dropped. Stubborn determination and unbridled curiosity, a deadly combination.

"Oh, shoot, I forgot something," Dusty said, already walking backward toward the arena. "I'll talk to you later, okay?"

Letty started to argue with her, but then just nodded with a look that said she knew only too well what Dusty was up to.

She thought again about the look she'd seen on Boone's face earlier and felt a shiver as she wandered back through the dark arena.

The outdoor arena looked alien with all the lights off, no crowds cheering from the empty stands, no bulls banging around in the chutes or cowboys hanging on the fences. Even the concession stands were locked up.

As Dusty headed toward the chutes, stars glittered in the dark sky overhead. The scent of dust, manure and fried grease still hung in the air. She felt a low hum in her body that seemed to grow stronger as she neared the chutes, as if the night were filled with electricity.

The same excited feeling she'd had the first time

she'd seen Boone Rasmussen a few weeks before. He'd been sitting on a fence by the bull chutes, his cowboy hat pulled low over his dark eyes. He'd taken her breath away and set something off inside her. Since then, Dusty hadn't been able to think straight.

Like now. If she had a lick of sense, she'd turn around and hightail it out of here. She heard the scuffle of feet in the dirt behind the chutes, a restless whisper of movement and saw a dozen large shapes milling inside a corral. The bucking horses.

The roughstock contractor hadn't finished loading up. That meant Boone could still be here since he had been working with Monte Edgewood, who provided the stock for the rodeo. Maybe Boone had stayed behind to help load the horses.

She climbed over the gate into the chutes. It was dark, but the stars and distant lights of the city cast a faint glow over the rodeo grounds. She moved along the chutes, stopping when she heard voices.

She looked past the empty corral and the one with the bucking horses and saw what appeared to be several cowboys. All she could really see were their hats etched against the darkness. Boone? She couldn't be sure unless she got a little closer.

Climbing over the fence, she dropped into an empty corral next to the one with the bucking horses. On the cool night breeze came the low murmur of voices. She felt her stomach roil as she tried to think of what she would say to Boone if that was him back there.

Unfortunately, she found herself tongue-tied whenever she saw him. She'd never had trouble speaking her mind. Quite the opposite. What the devil was wrong with her?

She knew she couldn't keep trying to get his attention the way she would have when she was ten. She had a flash of memory of her bucking horse ride earlier and Boone completely missing it. She still hurt from the landing. And the humiliation of her desperation.

Through the milling horses, she caught sight of the dark silhouette of three cowboy hats on the far side of the corrals. She couldn't see enough of the men to tell if one of them was Boone. It was too dark, and the horses blocked all but the men's heads and shoulders.

She stepped on one rung of the fence and tried to peer over the horses, surprised to hear the men's voices rise in anger. She couldn't catch the words, but the tone made it clear they were in a dispute over something.

She recognized Boone's voice and could almost feel the anger in it. Suddenly, it stopped. Eerie silence dropped over the arena.

Hurriedly she dropped back down into the corral, hoping he hadn't seen her, but knowing he must have. She felt her face flush with embarrassment. What if he thought she was spying on him? Or even worse, stalking him?

BOONE CAUGHT MOVEMENT beyond the horses in the corral and held up his hand to silence the other two.

A light shone near the rodeo grounds exit, but the arena and corrals lay in darkness. He stared past the horses, wondering if his eyes had been playing tricks on him. Through a break in the horses, he saw a figure crouch down.

"Go on, get out of here," he whispered.

Lamar nodded and headed for the semitruck and trailer with Devil's Tornado inside.

Boone glanced at Waylon Dobbs. The rodeo veterinarian looked scared and ready to run, but he hadn't moved.

"Who is it?" Waylon whispered.

Boone motioned with an impatient shake of his head that he didn't know and for Waylon to leave. "I'll take care of it. Go. We're finished here anyway."

Slipping through the fence into the corral with the bucking horses, Boone used the horses to conceal himself as he worked his way to the far gate—the gate that would send the massive horses back into the corral where he'd just seen someone spying on them.

Had the person heard what they'd been saying? He couldn't take the chance. Everyone knew accidents happened all the time when nosy people got caught where they didn't belong.

The horses began to move restlessly around the corral, nervous with him among them. His jaw tightened as he thought about who was just beyond the horses. He couldn't see anyone, but he knew the person was still there.

Carefully, he unlocked the gate and stepped back in the shadows out of the way of the horses. Whoever had been spying on him was in for a surprise.

Chapter Three

Ty Coltrane cupped his hands around his eyes and tried to see into the dark semitrailer. He could smell the bull, hear him breathing, but he couldn't see anything.

Unfortunately, there didn't seem to be anything to see. Devil's Tornado was so calm now that the bull had him doubting he'd seen anything unusual earlier.

Rodeo roughstock were raised to be as rank as possible. No one—not the bull rider, nor the audience—wanted a bull that didn't buck, that didn't put on show, that let the rider score big.

Devil's Tornado had done that and more.

So why had Ty stayed until the rodeo was over to sneak back here and get another peek at that bull? Because he couldn't forget what he'd seen in that bull's eyes. Or quit wondering what Rasmussen had done to the bull as it came down the exit chute.

But he wasn't going to find out anything tonight.

Earlier, he thought he'd heard voices over by the corrals, but hadn't been close enough to recognize them. When he'd been looking into the back of the semitrailer, he'd heard what sounded like the voices escalate into an argument.

But suddenly he realized that he couldn't hear them anymore. A sliver of worry burrowed itself under his skin. He didn't want to be caught back here snooping around the trailer. If he had reason to be suspicious, he didn't want Rasmussen or his cowboy thug getting wind of it.

He moved along the side of the trailer in time to see a short, squat figure moving toward a shiny black Lincoln. Veterinarian Waylon Dobbs.

The sound of the semitruck door opening made Ty jump. He peered between trailer and cab and caught a glimpse of Lamar Nichols a moment before the springs on the cab seat groaned under the big cowboy's weight. The semi's engine roared to life. Ty realized he'd be in clear view once the truck pulled away.

He glanced toward the horses in the corral and caught a glimpse of someone over by the gate. Boone Rasmussen.

In that instant, Ty felt a wave of apprehension as he realized that the voices he'd heard raised in argument had to have been those of veterinarian Waylon Dobbs, Boone Rasmussen and his employee, Lamar Nichols.

What the hell had they been arguing about? Devil's Tornado? Had the veterinarian seen what Ty had and confronted Rasmussen?

As Ty stared through the darkness past the horses,

he heard the faint squeak of a gate and realized Rasmussen had just opened the gate to let the large bucking horses back through toward the arena.

Now why would he do that?

The semitruck pulled away and Ty made a run for the corrals hoping Lamar wouldn't glance back.

Ty hadn't gone two feet when he saw Lamar's face reflected in the side mirror. The cowboy slammed on the semi's brakes as Ty slipped through the corral fence, disappearing into the dark.

DUSTY LISTENED, afraid to move. She heard the sound of the semitruck engine and what could have been another vehicle starting to leave. She waited, crouched in the darkness just inside the empty corral.

She felt like a fool. Could her timing be any worse?

The bucking horses in the next corral began to mill nervously, as if they were also aware of her presence.

She really needed to get out of here—hopefully, without being seen again. She tucked her long blond braid up under her western straw hat and tried to see through the moving horses. Dust rose around them. Her legs were starting to cramp. She leaned forward, one hand holding on to her leather-fringed shoulder bag, the other dropping to the soft earth. Her fingers felt something cold and hard in the dirt.

Dusty squinted down, shocked to see a used syringe lying in the dirt. What if one of the horses had stepped on it? Or one of the cows had eaten it? Carefully, she picked it up with two fingers and dropped it into her shoulder bag, planning to throw it away as soon as she reached the trash cans. She forgot about it almost at once as she heard a sound behind her.

She didn't dare turn and look. Straightening, she took a breath, rose and started back across the empty corral as if she weren't dying of embarrassment. Several of the horses snorted, and suddenly the whole bunch began to lap the adjacent corral behind her.

She winced, realizing she must have spooked them. Leticia had been right. She shouldn't have come back here looking for Boone. What had happened to her common sense?

She was halfway across the corral when she heard a gate groan open behind her. She turned, foolishly thinking all might not be lost. Maybe Boone had seen her and come after her. She tried to come up with a good excuse for being there.

But what she saw was the herd of huge bucking horses pour through the now open corral gate in a stream of pounding hooves, headed right for her.

Dusty started to run for the fence, her boots sinking in the soft turned earth. But she realized she wouldn't be able to reach it in time. She swung around, knowing the only way to keep from being trampled was to stand her ground.

As the horses thundered toward her, she waved her arms wildly, stomped her feet and yelled. The giant horses swelled around her, towering over her, the ground trembling under their weight, dust billowing up around them.

She could feel hot breath on the back of her neck as the dark shadows of the horses blocked any light from the stars above her. She waved, stomped and yelled as she edged back toward the fence.

A hand suddenly grabbed the back of her jean jacket and hauled her roughly up onto the rails as the horses circled the dark corral in a dusty stew.

She turned to face the man who'd just hauled her up on the fence, expecting to see Boone Rasmussen's handsome face.

"Ty?" she croaked, unable to hide her disappointment for the second time today. Ty Coltrane. "What are you doing here?" she demanded and shot a look past the corral. There was nothing but darkness where the three men had been earlier. In the distance, she heard the sound of vehicles leaving.

"How about, 'Ty, thank you for saving my skinny butt and not for the first time,'" he whispered, dragging her down off the fence. "Come on, let's get out of here."

She didn't argue. She could hear the horses racing around the corral behind her, which meant Boone would have a hard time getting them loaded now. If there was a chance he hadn't seen her…

She hightailed it through the space between the grandstands, glad for the darkness as Ty led her toward the nearly empty parking area.

"What were you doing back there?" Ty demanded once they were a good distance from the arena. He sounded like he always did after bailing her out of one of her messes. He was worse than one of her brothers.

"None of your business. Don't you get tired of following me around?"

It was too dark to see his blue eyes under the brim of his western straw hat. And she was glad of it. He shook his head at her as if he didn't know what to do with her. How about leaving her *alone?*

"My pickup's parked over there." He motioned toward the street and his black truck. Her tan ranch pickup was parked in the rodeo lot in the opposite direction. "Think you can make it home without getting into any more trouble?"

"I do just fine by myself, thank you very much." She mugged a face at him.

"Right."

She turned and stomped off toward her truck. It appeared to be the only one left in the lot. And to think earlier today she felt some semblance of affection for him.

As she neared the ranch truck, she realized there was another rig parked on the other side, all but hidden by the size of her truck. She quickened her step. Was it possible Boone had been out here waiting for her this whole time?

Rounding the front of the truck, she saw that it was only Leticia's yellow VW Beetle. Letty leaned against the car, waiting.

Dusty felt a surge of emotion to see that her friend had waited for her.

"Did you see Boone?" Letty asked.

Dusty shook her head.

"What happened? You look like you got rolled in the dirt," Letty said, straightening in alarm.

Dusty recounted her tale of woe as Ty made a circle through the empty parking lot, slowing as if he planned to follow Dusty home. But he sped up, seemingly relieved to see Letty with her.

"Was that Ty Coltrane?" Letty asked, as surprised as Dusty had been to see him earlier.

"*Yes.*" She brushed at the dirt on her jeans feeling foolish. "Just my luck, I run into Ty instead of Boone."

"What was Ty still doing there?" Letty asked as he left.

What *had* he been doing hanging around the rodeo grounds this late? Dusty shook her head, thinking instead about the men she'd heard arguing.

"You couldn't tell who the men were that Boone was arguing with?" Letty asked.

Dusty shook her head. "Boone's voice was the only one I recognized and I couldn't hear what he was saying." The sound of a large truck engine made them both turn to look toward the rodeo grounds again. A semi-truck left by the back way.

The night suddenly seemed darker. A quiet fell over the rodeo grounds. Only a few lights from town could be seen in the distance.

"I'd better get home." Letty started to get into her car, as if she were tired and did not want to hear any more about Boone.

Dusty couldn't blame her. She touched her sleeve. "Me, too." Things were weird enough at the ranch. Dusty didn't want her father worrying about her, and as long as she still lived in the main house… "Thanks for waiting for me."

Letty nodded and seemed to hesitate. "Sorry things didn't work out the way you'd hoped. Boone will come around."

Dusty smiled at her friend. Boone, she was beginning to realize, didn't just make her heart jump or her pulse pound. He made her crazy. No, she thought, he made her reckless, which right now seemed much worse. "Talk to you tomorrow."

Letty nodded and waited as Dusty got into the truck and started the engine. They'd brought separate vehicles because Letty had had to work late. Letty followed her all the way north as far as Antelope Flats before honking goodbye as she turned into the motel her parents had left her when they had retired.

Dusty continued north toward the ranch. Her disappointment hit her the moment she and Letty parted. She'd gone to the rodeo with such high hopes tonight.

She brushed at her tears of frustration. She hated feeling like this. Worse, acting like this.

Something flashed in her rearview mirror. She

glanced back to see a set of headlights as a vehicle came roaring up the highway behind her.

The headlights grew brighter, as if whoever was driving was trying to catch her. She couldn't imagine who it could be, unless Ty had been waiting to follow her home. That would be just like him.

She shook her head and sped up. Because of the hour, there were no other vehicles on the road. The lights behind her grew brighter and brighter. She glanced back in the rearview mirror, surprised how fast the vehicle was coming up on her.

The headlights were high, the rig definitely a pickup. That might have narrowed it down in any other place except the ranching town of Antelope Flats, Montana, where trucks outnumbered cars ten to one.

The truck was right behind her now. She flipped the rearview mirror up so the lights weren't blinding her. But she was still silhouetted in the glare of them.

Ahead, through her own headlights, she could see the county road turnoff. She waited, expecting the truck behind her to pass. But instead, it stayed right behind her.

She touched her brakes, hoping the driver would back off. But he didn't and she had the horrible feeling that he planned to force her off the road.

As the turnoff came up, she took the turn onto the county dirt road a little fast, fishtailing on the ruts. Behind her a wall of dust kicked up under her tires.

Forced to slow a little on the washboard dirt road,

she looked back and saw nothing but dust. She tried to relax, thinking she'd lost him. It had probably just been somebody with a few too many beers under his belt.

But she kept her speed up anyway. She knew this road, had driven it since she was twelve and had conned her dad into letting her get her license early, with the stipulation that she was only to drive on the ranch. That wasn't uncommon for ranch and farm kids in the state of Montana. What was uncommon was Asa McCall allowing it.

She hadn't realized how fast she was going until the pickup started to fishtail again on the washboard. Having driven more dirt roads than paved highway, she quickly got the pickup back under control and allowed herself to slow down a little.

In the distance, she could see the lights of the McCall ranch house and the turnoff to the ranch. Behind her, nothing but dust. Maybe.

She knew she'd have to slow down to make the turn onto the road down to the ranch, but once she did, she was sure no one would follow her up to the house. No one who knew the McCall men, anyway—and how protective they were.

Behind her, dust roiled up into the darkness. The entrance to the ranch road loomed in her headlights, the log arch, the sign: Sundown Ranch. Home. Safety. She'd never felt afraid here, didn't want to now.

She hit her brakes and cranked the wheel—glancing back as she did. The rearview mirror filled with headlights.

She swung through the ranch arch and onto the road that led to the ranch house, her pulse a war drum in her ears. The other rig had been right behind her!

Racing down the quarter-mile-long road to the house, she roared into the yard, shut off the engine and jumped out, ready to run as she looked back, half expecting to see the other rig coming after her. A few more stars had popped out, and there was just a sliver of moon.

As the dust settled, she felt her breath seize in her chest. A quarter mile back on the county road by the entrance to the ranch road, she could see the dark shape of a pickup, the headlights turned out. It was too far away and too dark to see who was behind the wheel. But the driver was sitting there in the darkness as if… Her heart began to pound furiously…as if watching her.

She turned and ran to the house. Racing up the steps and across the porch, she jerked open the door.

"What in the hell?" Asa McCall demanded as he came out of his den scowling at her. "I heard you come driving in. Are you drunk or just crazy, girl?"

"Someone followed me home." She pointed toward the road, shaking with fear.

Her father stepped out onto the porch and looked toward the gate. Asa was a big man with a reputation for being hard and uncompromising. Dusty knew he had a soft spot—at least where she was concerned. Soft spot or not, he would kill to protect his family.

"What are you talking about?" he demanded.

She moved to his side and followed his gaze. The dark shape of the pickup was gone, the road empty. "But he was just there."

"He?" Asa asked looking over at her.

"I just assumed it was a man," she said. "It was a pickup. Sitting up there by the gate with the headlights off. He chased me home."

Her father was still eyeing her. Dust hung like low clouds over the county road from where she'd raced home. Her father knew her, knew she didn't scare easily; he had to believe her.

"Was this some man you met at the rodeo?"

"No. I don't know who it was."

A muscle jumped in his jaw as he looked back out at the road. "I don't like you hanging around a rodeo this late at night."

"I was with Letty."

He glanced down at her as if sensing the truth. It was as if he could smell it on her.

"Ty Coltrane was there, too," she added quickly, knowing how much her father liked Ty.

He glanced back toward the road. "I'll take a look around in the morning."

She touched his arm as he turned to go back inside. "Thank you." She hadn't realized how much she'd needed him to believe her.

He smiled at her and cupped her cheek with one callused hand before he left her on the porch, the door closing behind him.

Dusty stood listening to the sound of his footfalls disappear down the hall as she stared at the ranch gate. The county road was empty, the pickup gone. Had he turned around and gone back to town? Or gone on up the road?

Someone had chased her home. But for what purpose?

She started out to the truck to get her shoulder bag, still unnerved. Had the driver planned to run her off the road or just follow her home? He'd definitely been trying to intimidate her.

She opened the pickup door and reached for her bag. Why would anyone follow her home unless…. Her heart thudded in her chest. Unless he wanted to see where she lived.

Clutching the leather pouch to her, she closed the truck door, telling herself that made no sense. All the person would have to do was mention her name and anyone in the county could tell him where to find the McCalls' Sundown Ranch.

McCall had always been an impossible name to live down, thanks to her four older brothers. They were to blame for how protective her father had always been with her. And the reason her teachers had warned her the first day of school that they weren't putting up with any more shenanigans from McCall kids.

She started up the front steps of the house and stumbled as a thought hit her. What if the driver of the pickup hadn't known who she was? Or where she lived?

Well, he did now, she thought with a shudder.

Chapter Four

Outside Antelope Flats

Sheriff Cash McCall slid down the steep embankment toward the partially hidden wrecked pickup lying in the bottom of the ravine. Coroner Raymond Winters waited in the shade of a chokecherry tree.

Winters was fifty-something, a quiet, mournful man who, besides being coroner for the county, owned Winters Funeral Home, just across the border in Sheridan, Wyoming.

The pickup had obviously rolled several times before coming to rest at the base of the tree. A rancher had spotted it while out on his four-wheeler checking calves and called 911.

As Cash neared the battered truck, he could see the Montana plates. Same county as Antelope Flats. He leaned into the cab, afraid he would know the driver.

He did.

"It's Clayton," Winters said behind him, sounding regretful. "Clayton T. Brooks. I saw him ride during Cheyenne Days. He was one hell of a bull rider. Damned shame. Heard he started hitting the bottle hard after he was forced to quit. That last bull broke him up good."

Cash nodded. Clayton T. Brooks was a legend in these parts. "They don't make 'em like him anymore," he agreed. What a hell of a way to end up, though, Cash thought.

Clayton was crumpled, beaten and broken on the floorboard on the passenger side of the pickup—and he'd been there for a while.

"Takes a certain kind of man to keep climbing back up on an animal that weighs a ton and would just as soon stomp you as not, don't you think?" Winters commented.

Unlike his brothers, and even his little sister Dusty, Cash had never rodeoed. Nor had he ever really understood the attraction. But then, he'd never been that much into ranching, let alone trying to ride animals intent on stopping you.

Cash tried the pickup door on the uphill side of the cab. Jammed. He went around, yanked on the other door. A dozen empty beer cans clattered to the ground.

"I would suspect his blood alcohol level was over the legal limit when he left the road," the coroner said dryly. "No skid marks up on the pavement. He didn't even try to hit his brakes. Wasn't wearing his seat belt, either."

"How long would you say he's been here?" Cash asked.

Winters shook his head. "Hard to say. My guess is at least a day, maybe more. I'll know more once I get him out of there."

Cash heard the whine of the ambulance siren.

"This has always been a bad curve," Winters said as the siren suddenly stilled, followed by the sound of doors opening and closing from the highway above them. "Looks pretty cut-and-dried. Alcohol-related fatality. Damned shame."

Cash agreed as he stepped back from the pickup, the smell of stale beer and death making him queasy this early in the morning. He turned to go up and help the ambulance crew with the stretcher, remembering the last time he saw Brooks.

The bull rider had been down at the Mint Bar with some of his drinking buddies. He'd been talking rodeo, all he ever talked about. It had been his life. Rodeo and the bulls he'd ridden. Clayton had been bragging about how he never forgot a bull.

As far as Cash knew, he had no family. But Clayton wouldn't be forgotten. The rodeo community would mourn his loss and he would go down in history as a cowboy who had ridden some of the most famous bulls in history during his career. Cash guessed that was more recognition than most people got after they were gone.

Still, it was a shame that Brooks couldn't have died doing what he'd loved instead of missing a curve on some dark stretch of narrow two-lane highway with too many beers under his last winning rodeo belt buckle.

DUSTY MCCALL BIT DOWN on her lower lip, hesitating as she looked toward the cool shaded entrance to the Coltrane Appaloosa Ranch barn.

For a moment, she almost turned around and rode back to her own ranch. But she'd come this far…

The sun was hot on her back. She slipped off her horse and sidled toward the barn door, stopping to peer in. There was still time to change her mind.

She could hear the low murmur of a male voice. Ty Coltrane's. She eased into the cool darkness, aware of something in the air. An electricity like static heat, taut with tension.

"Easy, pretty girl," Ty murmured from one of the horse stalls. "You're just fine. The first time is always the toughest."

Dusty edged deeper into the barn until she could peer over the top of the stall door. Ty sat on a bed of straw, his back to her and the stall door. In front of him a mare, her belly swollen to enormous proportions, paced in the confined space, her eyes on Ty, her expression worried.

In obvious agitation, the mare turned to her side to look back at her belly as if she felt the foal inside her and was confused by it. She stopped and nickered at Ty as if needing reassurance.

"It's all right," Ty murmured as he watched her. "That's it. Take your time. Nothing to be afraid of."

From experience, Dusty knew that most mares foal between midnight and 3 a.m. for some unknown reason. The fact that this mare was running late didn't bode well.

Dusty wasn't sure how long she stood there listening to Ty's soothing murmur and watching the pregnant mare, worrying that something was wrong.

Suddenly, the mare awkwardly lay down, her legs under her. With a groan, she went to her side.

Ty stroked the mare as he moved into position. From where Dusty stood she could see the foal start to appear. She stared at the purplish white bag covering the foal, trying see the new life inside it.

After a few minutes, she could make out the front hooves and then the head. The foal started out feet first, nose between its front legs as if diving. Then stopped.

Dusty stood transfixed, anxious now for the rest of the foal's body to be expelled. It was taking too long. She could feel Ty's nervousness as well as her own. She bit down on her lower lip, gripping the top of the stall door.

Ty rolled up his sleeves, still quietly encouraging, his hands and voice working to soothe the mare.

Nothing happened.

Dusty chewed at her lip, afraid as she watched him pull gently on the foal each time the mare pushed. It took everything in her not to go into the stall to help, but Ty was doing all that could be done and she didn't want to upset the mare.

Without warning the foal popped out—right into Ty's lap. He let out a surprised relieved laugh as he held the bundle.

Dusty felt her chest swell, tears burned her eyes as she watched Ty carefully brush back the white covering of the sack to let the gawky little thing breathe.

The foal had dark curly wet hair that looked like crushed velvet. As a ranchwoman, she'd seen dozens and dozens of births, but this one felt as if it were the most amazing. She gazed awestruck as Ty toweled the little colt dry, rubbing it gently, clearing away the protective cover, all the time murmuring to both. Talking softly, he rubbed the foal's ears, handled the hooves, flipped him over.

The mare watched. Dusty could feel the trust between the horse and Ty. He drew the foal over so the mare could tenderly nose it, smell it and as Dusty stared into the stall, the foal awkwardly got up on stick-like legs and stumbled to its feet, all legs and big eyes.

Dusty choked back a laugh. The foal nuzzled around the mare until Ty helped him get his first sips from one of the mare's two teats. The mare looked surprised for a moment, then seemed strangely content.

Dusty stared at the two horses standing next to each other, sensing the instinctive mother-child bond between them. She swallowed back the lump in her throat.

Ty turned, surprised to see Dusty McCall standing at the stall door, watching, her eyes wide and shiny as she stared down at the new foal.

As always, he felt that little flutter in his chest whenever he saw Dusty. He stepped out of the stall, closing the door as the mare began to clean up her new offspring.

"Hi."

Dusty didn't respond, seeming at a loss for words over the birth. He smiled at that. She never ceased to amaze him. After as many livestock as she'd seen birthed, she still got teary-eyed. He knew the feeling.

"It's just so incredible, isn't it?" she said after a moment.

He nodded. He'd seen more foals born than he could count, but he never got over the wonder of it.

He watched her peer into the stall, the expression on her face tender. He couldn't remember the last time she'd just dropped by like this. He had to wonder what she was doing here. Not that he was complaining. He liked her. He'd always liked her. Sometimes, he almost thought they were friends.

"It's just so…cool," she said, peeking over the stall door at the new foal again.

"It is that." He studied her, realizing she must have ridden over here. That's why he hadn't heard her drive up.

She was dressed in her usual: jeans, boots and one of her brother's cast-off western shirts under one of her brother's large cast-off canvas jackets, no makeup, her long blond hair plaited in a single braid down her back, her western straw hat pulled down low.

He had a sudden memory of her standing in the middle of the rodeo corral last night with wild bucking horses pounding around her. What the hell had she been doing there? After watching her ride one of the bucking broncs yesterday morning at the clinic, he wouldn't put anything past her.

"What are you going to name the foal?" she asked, finally looking over at him. She had the palest blue eyes he'd ever seen, peering out of gold dusted lashes.

He wondered what she saw when she looked at him. She usually treated him like one of her brothers—her least favorite, he thought with a wry smile.

"Haven't given a name any thought," he said. "What do you suggest?"

"Miracle," she said without hesitation. "What's his mother's name?"

"Rosie."

"Rosie's Little Miracle."

He laughed. "Great name for a roping horse." He pretended he was a rodeo announcer. "And our next contestant is Big Jim Brady on his horse Rosie's Little Miracle…" He laughed again.

Dusty mugged a face at him.

He headed deeper into the barn, needing to check several other mares that were due to foal. Unlike Rosie, though, those mares were old hands at this and wouldn't need any help. He'd been worried about Rosie. The first time was always the hardest.

Dusty followed him like one of the ranch dogs.

He stopped in front of a stall and she practically plowed into him. She hadn't just dropped by. The girl had something on her mind. He was dying to know what it was. "There something I can do for you, Slim?"

"Last night, did you go straight home from the rodeo?"

He raised a brow, amused. "You asking if I have myself a girlfriend in town?"

She rolled her eyes. "I just wondered, since you left before I did."

"Sorry to disappoint you, but I came straight here." He frowned. His horse ranch was down the county road from the McCalls' Sundown Ranch. "You rode all the way over here this early in the morning to ask me that? What's going on?"

She looked down as she dug the toe of her boot into the dirt and shook her head. "Nothin'."

He'd learned that *nothin'* with Dusty McCall was always *somethin'*. He leaned against the stall and crossed his arms. "Come on, what gives, Slim?"

She made another face at him. "I wish you'd quit calling me that."

He studied her. "Why do you care when I got home?"

She looked away, worrying her lower lip with her teeth the way she did when something was bothering her. "Someone followed me last night from town."

He felt his insides go cold. "What do you mean *someone?*" Last night, he'd seen Boone move through the bucking horses, heard him open the gate. At the time, Ty hadn't understood why Boone had sent the horses back through the empty corral—until Ty had hauled Dusty out a few moments later.

Had Boone known Dusty was in there? Or had he just heard someone and been afraid they'd overheard his argument with Dobbs and Lamar? Maybe Boone thought it was Ty in the corral spying on him. But that didn't explain what Dusty had been doing in there, did it?

"All I know is that whoever followed me was in a dark-colored pickup." She met his gaze. "Whoever was behind the wheel pretty much *chased* me home though."

"You mean like tried to run you off the road?" he asked, his mouth dry as straw.

"I never let him get that close."

Ty sighed, thankful Dusty was one kick-butt girl. "You couldn't tell the make or color of the pickup?"

"It was too dark." She cocked her head at him. "I just thought it might have been you because you're always turning up where I am. Like last night after the rodeo." Her big blue eyes narrowed. "What were you doing there anyway?"

"Well, I wasn't following you, Slim," he said, shoving off the stall door. "I need to get to work, even if you don't." He didn't like hearing that someone had followed her home. Any more than he liked hearing her complain about him always turning up around her.

"Well, you don't have to get mad."

He ground his teeth. Sometimes he wanted to ring Dusty McCall's slim neck. Other times…

It was the other times that had him walking away from her. She was just a kid. Just an annoying, pain-in-the-neck kid.

Dusty trailed after him until he stopped and spun on her. "I told you it wasn't me who followed you home."

"I believe you," she said, looking indignant.

"I could ask you what you were doing there," he said.

"I already told you. Nothing."

"Right. Well, now that we got that cleared up, is there something else I could help you with?"

"If you have to know, I left my bag and went back for it," she said.

He cut his eyes to her. "You left your bag in the horse corrals."

"I found it in the grandstand where I left it and then I wandered down to the horse corral."

He didn't believe a word of it. "Just to see the horses."

"No," she snapped. "I heard arguing. I was curious."

That, he believed. But something was bothering her. "Okay, Slim, spill it. Whatever it is, let's hear it."

She gulped air. "I need to ask your opinion on something." She swallowed and seemed to be having trouble finding her voice. A rare occurrence, considering how many times she'd told him what she thought in no uncertain terms. "It's kind of…personal."

Today he'd seen her wordless *and* choked up, all in

the same morning. And now she wanted to ask him something…personal?

She opened her mouth to speak, but closed it as a truck came up the road.

Ty swore under his breath when he recognized the rig. This didn't bode well, he thought, as the dark brown pickup pulled up in the yard and Boone Rasmussen climbed out.

"Stay here," Ty said to Dusty.

She didn't answer. Nor did she move.

As he stepped out of the barn, he glanced back. She was standing right where he'd left her, still as a statue. What the heck was going on with that girl, anyway? She never did what he told her. Hell, she did just the opposite to show him she didn't have to listen to him.

Except for just now.

Rasmussen got out of his truck and sauntered toward him, his face expressionless. Ty fought the bad feeling in the pit of his stomach.

Rasmussen had never been out to the Coltrane Appaloosa Ranch before. For that matter, he'd never acknowledged Ty, even though they'd met numerous times at rodeos. Every time they'd been introduced, Boone acted as if it had been the first, saying, "Coltrane? You raise…horses?"

Roping horses. Some of the best known in the world, including horses now being ridden by the top ropers in professional rodeo. But Boone Rasmussen knew that. Ty wondered why the man seemed to purposely rub him the wrong way. Or maybe that was just Boone Rasmussen's way. Whatever, Ty hadn't liked him. Didn't trust him. Especially after last night.

"Mornin'," Rasmussen said, glancing toward the barn, his gaze skimming over Dusty who stood silhouetted in the doorway, head down, her straw hat hiding her face. He shifted his dark eyes to Ty again without giving her another glance.

Ty waited, afraid he already knew what was on the cowboy's mind.

"I heard you raise horses," Rasmussen said, shoving back his hat.

"You know damned well I raise Appaloosa ropers."

Rasmussen's brow shot up. He pushed back his hat and smiled. "A little testy this morning, ain't we."

If he thought his good ol' Texas boy routine was going to work, he was sadly mistaken. "What is it you want, Rasmussen?"

"I was looking for a horse." He glanced toward the green pasture dotted with Coltrane Appaloosas.

Ty knew Rasmussen had no need of a roping horse. "You just missed our production sale. You might want to check it out next spring if you're still around. We'll have some yearlings and two-year-olds. The competition is pretty stiff, though."

Buyers came from all over the country. A Coltrane Appaloosa often went for thousands of dollars, especially progeny of one of his more famous roping horses with potential as breeding stock.

"But you're probably looking for a trained horse," Ty added. "Those go even higher and faster at the sale."

"I can train my own horse. And I will be around next spring." Rasmussen's jaw tightened. "You seem to have a burr under your saddle when it comes to me."

"You didn't come out here for a horse. What is it you're really after?"

"I could ask you the same thing." He glanced toward the barn again. Dusty was still standing in the same spot, hat down over her blue eyes, probably straining to hear their conversation. Ty doubted she could from this distance, but he knew she was damned sure watching them from under the brim of her hat. Slim was nothing if not nosy.

Rasmussen pulled off his straw hat and burrowed his fingers through his thick black hair. "What's your interest in my bulls?" he demanded, flicking a look at him.

"Who told you I was interested?" Ty asked, although he knew it was that rough-looking cowboy Rasmussen used in his chutes, Lamar Nichols.

"Doesn't matter. I just wondered why a man who raises roping horses would care about roughstock," Boone said. "You thinking of raising bulls?"

Ty wanted to laugh. Boone Rasmussen knew damned well that wasn't the case. "There a problem with me checking out your bulls?"

Boone shifted on his feet, looked down at his boots, then back up, the dark gaze boring into him. "Nope.

But if you're that interested I'd suggest you come out to the ranch in the daytime. Easier to see when it isn't pitch-dark."

"I just might take you up on that," Ty said. "The last time I saw a show like the one your bull put on last night was in Mexico."

Something dark and threatening flickered in Rasmussen's eyes before he looked away toward the barn. Ty followed his gaze. Dusty was gone.

For no reason he could put his finger on, Ty was relieved. She'd been near the corrals last night after the rodeo and had almost been trampled by the bucking horses, thanks to Rasmussen. Had she been snooping, too? More to the point, had Rasmussen seen her? Someone had followed her home. No, *chased* her home, she'd said.

Ty wanted to confront Rasmussen about opening that corral gate last night, but then that would mean involving Dusty and that was the last thing Ty wanted to do.

When Rasmussen looked at him again, Ty could feel rage coming off him in waves. They were about the same age, Rasmussen a few years older. Ty was a little taller and a little lighter, but he figured he could take Rasmussen in a fair fight. Except he doubted Boone Rasmussen had ever been in a fair fight in his life.

"You got quite the spread here," Rasmussen said, his voice sounding strange as if he were fighting to get some control over that rage. "Must be tough for someone your age. Have to keep your eye on things all the time. Probably don't have time to do much else."

Like snoop around rodeo arenas after dark? Ty heard the jealousy in Boone's tone and what sounded like a threat. He'd been running the Coltrane Appaloosa Ranch since his father's death two years ago. Rasmussen was right about one thing: it didn't leave much time for anything else.

"There a point you're trying to make?" Ty asked as he crossed his arms over his chest.

"Just making conversation."

"Well, if that's all, I've got some mares about to foal and don't really have time for conversation this morning."

Rasmussen flashed a smile that had no chance of reaching his dark eyes and tipped his hat. "I'm sure we'll be seeing each other again."

Count on it, Ty thought as he watched the cowboy get into his pickup and drive off.

Why had he driven all the way up here to begin with? Not for a horse, that was for sure. No, he wanted Ty to know that he knew about last night—knew Ty had been snooping around Devil's Tornado. And he'd come out here to warn him off.

This morning, Ty had half convinced himself that he'd been wrong about Devil's Tornado last night. That there wasn't anything to find out. Hell, hadn't Rasmussen invited him out to see the bulls in the daylight?

If there was something about Devil's Tornado that

Rasmussen didn't want him to see, then why make that offer?

It didn't make any sense.

So why was Ty even more convinced that Rasmussen had something to hide? Because he'd seen the cowboy's rage and something more. Boone Rasmussen had a mean streak that made him dangerous to anyone who got in his way.

And Ty had gotten in his way.

As he looked back toward the barn, Ty wondered if Dusty had also gotten in Boone Rasmussen's way.

Chapter Five

Shelby McCall was waiting for him when Asa came down to breakfast. They hadn't talked yesterday after his ride. He got the feeling she'd been afraid to ask him anything for fear he might tell her.

That wasn't like Shelby.

But one look at her face this morning told him everything he needed to know—even before she pulled the envelope from her apron pocket.

How ironic that his first thought was that he'd rather die than face her right now.

"When were you going to tell me?" Her voice quavered, eyes filling with tears but not falling, as if by her strength of will she could hold back the torrent.

He started to muddy the waters by demanding to know what she thought she was doing going through his things, but she would have seen right through that.

That day he'd gotten the letter, he'd been the one to go down to the mailbox at the end of the road. He'd seen her watching him from the window. He'd had to stuff the letter into his pocket to keep her from seeing it when he entered the house.

He smiled ruefully now. Of course she would have noticed. He couldn't get anything past her. Never could.

"Where did you find the letter?" he asked, stalling.

She gave him an exasperated look. "In your jacket pocket where you put it. Not that it matters where I found it. *Asa.*" The pain in her voice was heart-wrenching, but he could tell she was trying to be strong for him. For the children. "You have to tell them."

He nodded as he pulled out a chair at the kitchen table and lowered himself into it. He couldn't remember ever feeling so bone-weary.

"There's more," he said, his voice sounding hoarse even to his own ears. He looked up at her.

She straightened to her full height, head going up, that stubborn determined look in her beautiful face as she took the chair across from him. "Tell me."

"It's rather a long story."

"I have time," she said, then seemed to bite her tongue. One errant tear spilled over her cheek. She hurriedly wiped it away and met his gaze, still refusing to acknowledge something they'd both known for a long time.

He was dying.

The letter only confirmed what he'd suspected. For him, time had run out.

TY FOUND Dusty by Rosie's stall. She stood on tiptoe, peering in at the new foal she wanted to name Miracle. Her expression was so tender he felt his heart do a slow painful somersault in his chest.

It surprised him she hadn't come out of the barn when Rasmussen was here. It wasn't like her. Normally, she would have been right in the middle of the conversation. Strange, she had almost seemed...shy.

He shook his head at such a thought. This was Dusty McCall, he reminded himself. Dusty and shy didn't go together.

But was it possible she was scared of Rasmussen?

"What did Boone want?" Dusty asked as she glanced toward the barn door. Dust still hung in the air from the trail his pickup had left behind.

"Nothin'," Ty said. She looked pale to him. He watched her burrow down into her jacket. "You all right?"

"I'm fine."

"Any reason you didn't want to see Rasmussen just now?" he asked.

She gave him a surprised, wide-eyed look. "I've never even met him, just know who he is. Anyway, you told me to stay here."

Ty studied her. *She never does what I tell her.* He sighed. "What was it you were going to ask me before he showed up?"

She looked away. "It wasn't important."

"Fine. Whatever." Turning, he headed down between the stalls. He'd never understand that girl. He checked the mares again, mentally noting that he might have to call in a couple of his hands if the mares decided to foal at the same time, just to keep an eye on them in case anything went wrong.

Still no word from Clayton. He was torn between worry and annoyance. Mostly worry. No one seemed to have heard from him for several days.

Ty turned, surprised to find Dusty had followed him. "I thought you left." He didn't know what was bothering her, but she was starting to irritate him. He knew Dusty too well. Something was on her mind and he was getting tired of waiting to hear what it was.

He thought of Rasmussen and was reminded again that Dusty had almost been trampled by the bucking horses last night. Just the thought made his stomach churn. He told himself that Dusty had just been in the wrong place at the wrong time last night. But if he was right about Boone Rasmussen, then he didn't want Dusty anywhere near the man. Or his roughstock.

"Last night after the rodeo, you didn't happen to hear what Boone and his buddies were arguing about, did you?" he asked, thinking that might be the problem.

She shot him a surprised look. "No. Why?"

"Just curious," he said and wished he hadn't said anything. She was giving him that fish-eye look of hers and he could almost see the wheels turning in her head.

"Is that what you were doing there? Trying to hear what they were saying?"

"I stayed around to see one of the bulls." He turned to walk away from her, hoping she dropped it.

But then that wouldn't have been like her.

"Why would you want to see one of Boone's bulls?" she demanded, trailing after him. "The two of you didn't seem all that friendly a few minutes ago."

He spun on her. "Was there some reason you came up here today other than to give me a hard time?"

She seemed to deflate before his eyes. She let out a sigh. "There's something I need to know." She sighed again. "You're a man."

He let out a laugh. "Last time I checked."

She rolled her eyes. "You know what I mean."

He didn't really, but she'd definitely gotten his interest. Where in the world was she headed with this, though? He gave her his full attention as he waited to see.

"Do you think I'm…*cute?*" She practically choked on the word.

"Cute as a button," he said meaning it, relieved beyond words that this was all she wanted to know.

She swallowed and bit her lower lip, lowering her eyes. "I mean do I turn you on?"

"I beg your pardon?"

"Oh, I knew you were the wrong one to ask." She spun around and stalked toward the barn door.

He went after her, grabbing her arm and spinning her around so he could see her face. Damned if she wasn't crying. He let go of her in surprise. "Talk to me, Slim."

She made an angry swipe at her tears. "Do you have any idea what it's like being raised on a ranch far from anything in an all-male family? I've spent my whole life trying not to be different. I just wanted to fit in, and that meant trying to be just like my brothers."

He raised a brow. "I don't think being a tomboy is a bad thing, Slim. Hell, you can ride better than most men and before your brothers Rourke and Brandon started helping, you and J.T. were running the Sundown spread."

She windmilled her arms and let out an exasperated breath. "I'm not saying I don't love ranching. And I never wanted to be one of those prissy girls like you've dated." She made a face. "It isn't about that."

He waited, trying not to comment on her jab about the prissy girls he'd dated.

"It's about *sex,*" she said on a breath and looked down at her boots.

Ty reared back. "Wow. Slim, if this is about the birds and bees, then you should be talking to your mama."

She mugged a face at him. "I've known about sex since I was old enough to peer through the fence at the cattle."

"Then you've lost me," he said just wanting this conversation to be over.

"Lately, I've been having these…*feelings,*" she said, her head down again.

Ty let out a nervous laugh. Oh, brother.

"I should have known you wouldn't help me."

As she started to stomp off, he reluctantly grabbed her arm again. "Look, I'd help you if I could. It's just that this is the kind of thing you discuss with your mother or a friend."

"I can't talk to Shelby about anything."

He knew that Dusty was still having trouble accepting her mother. Shelby McCall had only recently returned after being gone most of her children's lives— all of Dusty's.

"And I thought you *were* my friend," she accused, eyes narrowing.

He took off his hat and shot a hand through his hair. "I was thinking more of a *girl*-type friend."

"Letty?" she cried.

Letty, who was even more of a tomboy than Dusty, probably had less experience with this type of thing than Slim. "You have a point. What about your sisters-in-law?"

"I hardly know them and they're…old."

He smiled at that. Her sisters-in-law were all in their thirties. "Okay," he said before she could take off again. He was five years her senior. Did she see him as "old" too?

He groaned at the thought. The problem was: he'd never seen her like this. Sure, he'd seen her upset. Usually after she'd been bucked from a horse. Or tossed into a mud puddle by one of her brothers when she was younger. But this was different, and he knew he couldn't just let her leave thinking he wasn't taking her seriously.

"Come over here," he said and pulled down a straw bale for her to sit on. He dragged up one for himself and sat facing her. "What brought this on, anyway?"

She bit down on her lower lip, eyes down, then slowly raised her lashes, those blue eyes huge in the cool darkness of the barn and swimming with tears. "I'm *twenty-one*. I'm tired of being treated like a kid."

Twenty-one. He stared at her, realizing it was true. He hadn't even thought about how old she was, even though he'd known her since they were kids. She'd always just been the girl next door—well, the tomboy down the road at the next ranch, anyway. He'd pretty much always thought of her as a kid.

On top of that, she still *looked* like a kid. For starters, she was only about five-five, lean and youthful-looking. But he knew it was more than that. She was the kid sister of the very protective McCall boys. That alone made any man with any sense shy away from her. Just as that alone should have made him nervous about having this conversation with her.

"Have you mentioned this to your brothers?" he asked.

She rolled her eyes and shot to her feet. "Just forget it."

"Hold on," he said, pulling her back down to the straw bale. "I'm not sure I'm the right person," he said, adding quickly before she tried to hightail it again, "but I'll help you if I can."

"You do know *something* about women, don't you?"

He smiled. "Something."

Her blue eyes pleaded with him. "Well, then help me. I want people to see me as a…woman."

Oh, man, Slim. He told himself that she wouldn't be here asking him—of all people—unless she was desperate. "Okay," he said uncomfortably. "Don't take this wrong, but it could be the way you dress."

She looked down at her clothes. "What's wrong with the way I dress?"

"Well, for starters, you look like a boy. You have any of your own clothes? Or is everything you own handed down from your brothers."

Her jaw tightened. "I like roomy shirts."

He nodded. Either she was wearing a tight-fitting sports bra under one of her brother's western shirts and canvas jacket or she had no boobs and didn't even need a bra. "Don't you ever look at magazines? Or try makeup and fixing your hair different?"

"*Of course.* I looked like a streetwalker!" She let out a half sob, half laugh. A couple of big tears shimmered in her blue eyes. She ducked her head again, obviously embarrassed as she made a swipe at them. "I need one of those makeovers like on TV."

He shook his head. "You don't need a makeover. You just need a little help. Look, if you're serious about this—"

"I am."

"—then I'll help you," he said with a groan.

The relief in her face made him smile. Then realization hit him. What did he know about girl stuff? Clearly more than Dusty, which wasn't much. Fortunately, he knew someone he could get to help them, a young woman he'd dated a few times who owned a boutique in Sheridan.

"We'll go down to Sheridan."

She stood as if ready to go right now.

He wondered what the hurry was. "Can you go this afternoon?"

She nodded, looking determined and a little worried.

"I'll pick you up after lunch."

She launched herself at him. He hugged her back in surprise and then she was racing toward the barn door. He smiled, thinking he didn't see any reason for her to change. Personally, he liked her just fine as a tomboy.

Over her shoulder, she called back, "If you tell a soul about this—"

"It will be our little secret," he said, getting up to follow her to the barn door. No chance he was going to tell anyone.

She swung up onto her horse outside the barn and cut her eyes at him. "It had better be our secret, Ty Coltrane, or you will regret the day you ever met me."

No chance of that, he thought as he watched her ride away. He'd never met anyone like Slim. She was one hell of a horsewoman. And she had spunk and something he couldn't put his finger on. Something that had always drawn him to her. Yep, as far as he was concerned, there was nothing about Dusty McCall that needed to be made over.

As she disappeared over the horizon, he turned back to the barn. A bad feeling settled over him as he thought again of Rasmussen's visit and Dusty's.

What *had* Dusty been doing in the corral last night after the rodeo?

ASA HAD KNOWN the day would come when he would have to tell his family. Telling them he was dying seemed easy compared to the really bad news. Telling Shelby took ever ounce of strength he had left in him.

"Remember Charley Rankin?" he asked.

She frowned. "The two of you owned that land together to the north."

Asa nodded. "Charley helped me buy up some other prime acreage that is now part of the main ranch. I bought the land from him when we dissolved our partnership."

"That must have been when Charley married and moved back east."

Asa nodded, realizing not for the first time that Shelby had kept close track of his life and the kids all the years he'd forced her out of their lives. It added to the weight of his guilt to know that she'd been watching them all from the sidelines, staying involved in their lives as much as she could. As much as he'd allowed her.

He met her eyes, wanting desperately to tell her how sorry he was but never able to find words to encompass the extent of that sorrow—of that regret.

Ashamed, he looked away.

"I heard Charley and his wife were both killed when his private plane crashed," she said when he didn't go on.

He nodded and plunged in, needing to get the words out before he didn't have the courage. "When our partnership was dissolved, I didn't have enough cash to buy him out, so I signed an agreement giving him the mineral rights to the ranch."

She let out a small gasp, her eyes widening with alarm as the enormity of what he'd done hit her.

"It was collateral, nothing more," he continued, not wanting to drag it out. "Just before he was killed, I mailed the last of the land payments. Charley had never cashed the checks. He didn't need the money, so I guess it was his way of helping me out. With the last check, I also sent him a legal form to sign that would void the mineral rights agreement."

He looked at Shelby. He could tell by her expression that she knew what was coming.

"Charley and his wife had a son," she said. "Reese. He must be about twenty-five by now."

Asa nodded, figuring Shelby also knew that Reese had never gotten along with his father and been in trouble since he was young. "He found all the paperwork on the deal after his father's death, including all the uncashed checks and the unsigned document that would have voided the agreement."

"Oh, Asa," she breathed.

He nodded. "Thanks to the discovery of coal-bed methane, the mineral rights on the ranch are worth fifty times what I paid Charley for the land."

"He plans to drill wells on the ranch." Shelby covered her mouth with her hand, eyes welling with tears. She knew better than anyone how much this ranch meant to him.

She pushed herself up from the table and went to the window, her back to him. "There has to be some way to stop him."

"Even if I mortgaged the entire ranch, there wouldn't be enough capital to buy him off. He always resented Charley. Charley's dead. But Charley's best friend is still alive. At least for a while."

She turned from the sink and sat down at the table again. Reaching across the table, she covered his weathered old hand with her still pale pretty one. "Have you told J.T.?"

J.T. was their oldest, the one who had been running the ranch along with Dusty the past few years. Asa shook his head. "Other than my lawyer, you're the only one who knows."

"You have to tell them."

He turned his hand so hers was enclosed in his rough weathered one. He squeezed it gently as he looked at her. He'd been so angry at her for coming back from the dead the way she had. Breaking their agreement without notice. Just showing up at the door. Giving him no choice but to let her stay because she'd learned about the cancer.

Then when it had gone into remission, she'd stayed, refusing to leave him again. He'd been angry at her, not wanting her pity. Not wanting her to come home only to watch him waste away and die.

Now he wondered what he would have done if she hadn't come back. How he and the children would have gotten through this without her here. How could he ever tell her how much it meant to him? How much she meant to him?

"You have to tell the children," she said again.

He nodded. The cancer was no longer in remission. The letter had only confirmed what he'd already known.

He drew his hand back and stood. His eyes burned at just the thought of leaving her and the children with the mess he'd made. "I need a little more time."

It was so like Shelby not to say that he might not have more time. "Take all you need."

He smiled ruefully at that. He would need another lifetime and even then, he doubted it would be enough time to undo all the mistakes he'd made in this one.

Instead, he had a few weeks. If he was lucky.

Chapter Six

Letty Arnold stared at the caller ID as the phone rang again. She'd been waiting for this call all her life. She just hadn't known it.

Her hand shook as she picked up. She crossed her fingers and closed her eyes. "Hello?"

"Ms. Arnold?"

She held her breath, squeezing her eyes tighter.

"This is Hal Branson with Branson Investigations."

She recognized his voice from the day she'd hired him. The same day she'd found out from the sheriff that she'd been illegally adopted.

The truth about her adoption had only come out because of an investigation involving a local doctor. It seemed he'd taken babies from what he considered unworthy parents, telling them that their infant had died. Then he had given the babies to couples desperately wanting a child, couples he considered more worthy.

The doctor had handled everything, including birth certificates that made it appear the new mother had given birth to the baby. If he hadn't told the sheriff about her in a deathbed confession, she might never have known the truth. "Did you find my birth mother?"

"Maybe," Hal Branson said.

Letty opened her eyes. "*Maybe?*"

"I found a woman who gave birth to a baby at the clinic where the doctor worked on the day you were supposedly born." He seemed to hesitate. "She was an unwed mother." Just the kind of woman the doctor would have considered unworthy. "I don't want to get your hopes up. The only way to be certain of your maternity will be DNA tests."

He'd already told her all of this. Why was he telling her this again?

"Keep in mind that the date of your birth could be incorrect," he continued. "You could have been a home birth. There are just too many factors. And with the doctor not keeping any records of the adoptions—"

"Mr. Branson—"

"Hal." He sounded young and she wondered how old he was. For all she knew, she'd hired a kid. That's what she got for not taking care of this in person. Not that she hadn't checked out Branson Investigations on the Internet to make sure it was licensed, bonded and reputable.

She hadn't wanted anyone in Antelope Flats to know that she was one of the crazy doctor's "babies." And she hadn't had the patience that day to drive clear to Billings to find a P.I. It was also easier to talk about this over the phone rather than in person.

She knew she shouldn't feel this way, but it was embarrassing not knowing who her parents were. Not knowing who *she* was.

And she had to know. She'd always suspected that she didn't really belong to the Arnolds. It wasn't only their advanced ages and the fact that they were more like grandparents. She'd never looked like either of them or acted like them or even really understood them. The Arnolds were quiet, solitary, stable and bland. Both were short and round.

Letty was thin as a stick, with a wide toothy smile, and had been all cowgirl from the time she could walk. Neither of her parents had ever ridden a horse in their lives and didn't like rodeos. And while both of the Arnolds had light brown hair, Letty had a wild mane of hair red as a flame, a face full of freckles and emerald green eyes. Both Arnolds had brown eyes.

The truth? She'd been relieved when they'd retired and left her the motel so they could move to Arizona. Not that they hadn't been good to her. She *loved* them.

That's why she felt guilty about her feelings. They were the only parents she'd known and she felt as if she were disrespecting them by even looking for her birth mother.

"Are you still there?" Hal asked.

"Tell me how I can find this woman you think might be my birth mother." Letty unconsciously glanced toward her reflection in the mirror on the wall. She had to know who she was. No matter the outcome.

"Her name is Florence Hubbard. She goes by Flo."

Letty heard the slight catch in his voice and braced herself.

"She…plays in a rock 'n' roll band," Hal said. "It's called Triple-X-Files. I understand they play some rock, but mostly heavy metal music."

She could hear his distaste and smiled. "What kind of music do you like?"

"What?" He sounded more than surprised, maybe even embarrassed. "Country," he said almost sheepishly.

Her smile widened. "Me, too. So where does this X band play?"

"Well…there's a three-day rock concert next weekend during a fair in Bozeman. Triple-X-Files will be there. If you like, I could e-mail you all the information. You can camp near the concert or stay in one of the local motels."

"Thanks, you've been very thorough."

"It's what you're paying me to do." Again, he sounded embarrassed.

"You'll send me a bill?" she said, thinking this might be the last time they talked if Flo Hubbard really was her mother.

"Ms. Arnold—"

"Letty."

"Letty, if I were you, I wouldn't go to meet this woman alone. Do you have a friend or relative who could go with you?"

She smiled ruefully at the relative part. None who lived nearby, none she was all that close to even before she found out they weren't blood-related. She had no one who could go with her. Except Dusty McCall, her best friend.

But she wasn't ready to tell even Dusty about this yet. Dusty knew something had been bothering her. Letty wished she could confide in her friend. She wasn't even sure what was holding her back. Maybe the need to find out who she was before she told the world that she was one of the babies the doctor had stolen.

"If you would like, I could meet you there," Hal said guardedly. "I mean, I wouldn't mind. In fact, I think it might be good to have someone who isn't involved in the situation there with you."

To her surprise, she heard herself say, "Would you?"

"Of course." He sounded relieved, almost excited, as if he wanted to see this through to the end. "Just tell me when and where to meet you."

They worked out a plan and she found herself torn between her anxiety at the thought of meeting her possible birth mother and her curiosity about Hal Branson as she hung up.

For a moment, she thought about calling Dusty, telling her the news. She hesitated, feeling guilty. But the truth was, Dusty hadn't been interested in much of anything lately except Boone Rasmussen.

Letty told herself that wasn't fair. She knew Dusty

would just think she was jealous. But it was something else that bothered her about Dusty's obsession with Boone. A fear that she might lose her best friend. But not to love.

BOONE RASMUSSEN STORMED into Monte Edgewood's ranch house, letting the door slam behind him. Hadn't he known Coltrane was going to be a problem? The Coltranes of the world were always a problem.

The ten-mile drive from Coltrane's ranch hadn't calmed him in the least. He'd driven too fast on the way to Monte's, reckless from his anger. How dare Coltrane butt into his business?

Coltrane had everything Boone had ever wanted— one hell of a ranch, money, standing in the community—and all of it handed to him on a silver platter when his old man died.

Boone hadn't been so lucky. His father hadn't left him a thing. In fact, he'd had to pay out of his own pocket to have the old son of a bitch cremated. He smiled bitterly at the memory. He should have let the state deal with G.O. Rasmussen's sorry remains.

But Boone had gotten the last laugh. He'd spread that bastard's ashes over the local cow lot. Ashes to ashes, so to speak. It was little consolation for the years his old man had worked him, paying him with biting criticism and the back of his hand, but it was something.

The difference in their lives alone made Boone hate

Coltrane. But now the horse rancher was snooping into the wrong cowboy's life. No way was he going to let Coltrane ruin everything he'd worked so hard for.

Monte looked up from the kitchen table. Boone saw the older man's expression and felt his stomach clench. Something *else* had happened. Something to do with Devil's Tornado? Or did this have something to do with Coltrane?

Monte lowered his big head as if in prayer. "I guess you heard about Clayton," he said with a wag of his head.

Boone tried not to let Monte see his relief. So this was only about that ranting old drunk bull rider. He thought for a moment of pretending he hadn't heard, but everyone in town was talking about Clayton's death.

"I heard," Boone said, drawing up a chair at the table and sitting down, trying to mirror Monte's sorrowful expression. "Did you hear what happened?" Monte had more reliable sources than Boone did.

"His body was found in a ravine south of here. Guess he missed a curve," Monte said.

"Probably blind drunk."

Monte gave him a hard look, disappointment shining in his light eyes. "Shouldn't speak ill of the dead, son. Clayton had his share of demons like all of us, but he was a good man." He reached across the table to drop a big palm on Boone's shoulder and gave it a squeeze as he smiled sadly. It was clear to both of them that Boone would never be the man Monte had hoped.

But Monte refused to give up on him.

And that was what Boone was counting on.

With each passing day, though, the stakes got higher and higher. So did the danger of being caught.

Sierra sashayed into the room. "What's going on? You look like you lost your best friend."

Monte gave her an indulgent smile and motioned for her. She stepped into his open arms, stroking his hair as she looked across at Boone.

"A bull rider I admired died in a car accident," Monte told her. "Clayton T. Brooks. He was quite the rodeo star in his day."

"That's too bad," Sierra said, her gaze heating up as her eyes locked with Boone's.

Boone pushed to his feet. "Need anything from town?"

Monte shook his head, dropping his gaze again to the table as Sierra stepped away from him. He looked old and tired, and more upset over Clayton than Boone would have expected. It made Boone wonder how well the two had known each other. And if that was a problem he should be worrying about.

He shoved that worry aside and concentrated on a more immediate one. Judging from her size, it had been a cowgirl he'd seen in the empty corral next to the bucking horses last night after the rodeo. A lucky cowgirl who'd somehow escaped being trampled by the bucking horses.

Coltrane had fished her out of the corral. Boone had

seen the two head for the parking lot. Then he'd lost sight of them. At first, Boone had been worried that she'd overheard him and Lamar arguing with Waylon Dobbs. That alone would have been a loose end he couldn't afford.

But he'd seen the cowgirl reach down in the horse corral and pick up something from the ground. His hand had gone to his jacket pocket. The syringe was gone! It must have fallen out of his pocket when he'd climbed over the corral fence earlier.

He'd seen her put it in her purse! It made no sense. Why had she been there in the first place? Why put a used syringe into her purse?

"Pick me up some ice cream if you're going to town," Sierra said.

"I'll buy you some ice cream, sugar," Monte spoke up.

Boone glanced back at Monte, trying to read his expression. Monte met his gaze and for an instant, Boone thought he saw something he didn't like flicker in the older man's gaze. Just his imagination?

Well, there would be plenty of time to deal with Monte later—if it came to that.

And Sierra too, he thought stealing a look at her as he left.

DUSTY PACED on the porch, mentally kicking herself for asking for Ty's help. What had she been thinking? Surely she wasn't *that* desperate.

At first, all she saw was the dust on the county road. Her heart lodged in her throat as Ty turned onto the road to the ranch. She would tell him she'd changed her mind. Didn't women do that all the time?

She groaned, reminding herself why she *was* so desperate for a makeover to begin with. But desperate enough to see this through with Ty, of all people?

He pulled up in the yard and she ran out, jerked open the passenger side door of his pickup and jumped in before she could change her mind—or he could get out.

He looked over at her and slammed his partially opened door.

"What?" she asked seeing his annoyed expression.

"You might have given me a chance to open your door for you," he said.

She rolled her eyes. "You have to be kidding. Does anyone do that anymore?"

"I do when I come by to pick up a woman," he said, sounding indignant.

She cut her eyes at him. "Why?"

"Because it's polite."

"I can open my own door."

"That isn't the point," he said as he shifted the pickup into gear and started out the gate. "Look, think of dating as a game between men and women with certain rituals involved. There are steps a man and woman go through in the relationship. Certain roles each sex plays."

She groaned. "Why does it have to be so complicated? Why can't we just cut to the chase? Be honest? Tell the person how we feel? Have them tell us how they feel? And if we both feel the same..."

Ty laughed and shook his head. "Sorry, Slim, but it doesn't work that way. It's the anticipation, not knowing what's going to happen, that adds to the excitement."

She thought about Boone. She wanted to know what was going to happen. She couldn't stand the suspense.

"It's all part of the mating ritual. You just need to get into your role."

Dusty scoffed. "This role you're talking about. Tell me it doesn't mean I have to act helpless because I'm never going to be one of *those* women," she informed him haughtily. "So if that's what I have to do, forget it." She could feel him studying her out of the corner of his eye as he drove.

He laughed. "No, you're never going to be one of those. Lucky for you, there are men who actually like strong independent women. But no man may be ready for *you.*"

She punched his arm but laughed with him, then turned to gaze out at the countryside. Was Boone ready for her? White billowing clouds scudded through the summer-blue sky overhead, casting pale shadows over the red rock cliffs, the silken ponderosa pines and tall, dark-green grasses. The land stretched to the horizon. McCall land.

Dusty welled with pride, never tiring of the landscape. This was her home. Her mother and father hadn't understood why nothing could dislodge her from the isolated ranch.

A few months ago, Shelby had cornered her, questioning her about her future. "You need to go to college," her mother had insisted. "You need a good education."

"I have a good education," Dusty had snapped. "Not that you would know, but I graduated from high school early and have been taking college courses for years online. I'll have at least two degrees, one in business and another in agriculture by this time next year."

"I'm aware of that," Shelby said tightly. "But it's not the same as actually attending a university, meeting other people your age, broadening your horizons."

Dusty had laughed. "Look at my horizons," she'd said widening her arms to encompass the ranch. "They're plenty broad."

"What do you have to say?" Shelby had asked turning to her husband.

Asa had studied Dusty for a long moment. "Dusty's always known her own mind. Much like her mother," he'd added, his gaze shifting to Shelby. "I've never been able to change either of your minds. And God knows, I've tried."

Dusty had seen the look that passed between her parents. There was little doubt they had a secret, one she and her brothers obviously weren't privy to.

She'd never regretted her decision to stay on the

ranch. Her father had given her some acreage to the south and told her she could build a house on it someday if she wanted to—now, or when she got married. Unless the man she married wanted to live elsewhere.

She had laughed. "I wouldn't marry anyone who wanted to leave here. Don't you know me better than that?"

Her father had frowned. "You haven't been in love yet. Love changes everything."

She had scoffed at the idea. But now as she watched the land blur by, she thought of Boone Rasmussen. Was this love? She felt all jittery inside. Her heart beat out of control half the time. And it made her unsure about everything. Especially herself. Was that love?

Ty turned onto the highway. Dusty's shoulder bag rolled off the seat, hitting the floor with a loud thump.

"What have you got in there? Bricks?"

"Stuff. A bridle I need to get repaired. Books," Dusty said scooping the heavy bag up from the floor. "Sometimes I want to read when I have to go into town on errands for the ranch. There's nothing wrong with reading."

He laughed. "I didn't say there was." They passed through Antelope Flats, the small Montana town quickly disappearing behind them.

Dusty reached over and turned on the radio, not surprised to find it tuned to a country-western station. Leaning back, she watched the willow-choked Tongue River twist its way through the valley as she and Ty wound south toward Wyoming, not wanting to talk. She had a lot on her mind.

"Did you find out who that was who followed you home last night?" Ty said reaching over to turn down the radio.

She shook her head, the memory still making her uneasy. "Just a dark-colored pickup. The driver stopped at the ranch gate and sat there with his headlights out for a while. The next time I looked, he was gone. It was probably nothing." She wished she could believe that.

She saw Ty's concerned expression. The last thing she wanted was Ty Coltrane keeping an eye on her. He'd done that her whole life.

"Any chance it could have been Boone Rasmussen?" he asked.

The question took her by surprise. "Why would *he* follow me?"

Ty looked over at her. "Good question. Maybe because you were spying on him last night in the horse corral. I heard him open that gate. It was no accident that you were almost trampled by those bucking horses."

She stared at him in shock, remembering the sound of the gate latch being pulled back, the gate swinging open.

"That's crazy. Why would Boone want to hurt *me?* He doesn't even know who I am."

Ty lifted a brow. "Maybe. Or maybe he thought you overheard something you shouldn't have last night."

The thought chilled her. "I didn't hear *anything*."

"But maybe Boone doesn't know that. Just be careful, okay?" His tone was relaxed enough, but she could tell he was anything but. "Stay away from Boone Rasmussen."

She cut her eyes at Ty. Did he know the real reason she was in that corral last night? Was he just trying to keep her away from Boone? A thought struck her. Was it possible Ty was…jealous? She rejected that explanation instantly. No, Ty was just playing big brother like he always had.

"You never told me why *you* were there last night," she said. Did it have something to do with Boone and why Boone had stopped by Ty's ranch this morning?

From the barn, she hadn't been able to hear what the two had been saying to each other, but she could darn well tell by reading their body language that they'd been at odds over something. Could it have been about *her?*

"Well?" she demanded when Ty didn't answer her.

"Settle down, Slim. What do you want me to say? That I saw your truck was still in the lot and figured you were in some kind of trouble, as usual? That when I heard arguing, I just assumed you were at the center of it?"

She angled a look at him. He didn't take his eyes off the road making her suspect there was more to it.

Didn't he realize that trying to keep a secret from her was like throwing a rodeo bullfighter at a bull? Especially since whatever Ty was hiding had something to do with Boone Rasmussen.

Boone wouldn't have purposely opened the corral gate. But she had a flash of memory: the expression on Boone's face when he'd reached through the chute toward Devil's Tornado. She shivered, hugging herself. Ty turned on the heat in the pickup, but this chill went bone-deep.

If Boone had opened that corral gate, then it had been to scare her away. But then she had to wonder what he'd been arguing about with the two other men that he'd feared she'd overheard.

JUST NORTH OF Antelope Flats, Boone Rasmussen turned onto a dirt road that wound down to the Tongue River Reservoir. The beat-up, older model truck and camper were parked next to the water near the dam.

As Boone got out, he saw no sign of life, but a pile of crushed beer cans glinted in the sun outside the camper. He swore under his breath as he pounded on the door and waited. Inside, he could hear rustling. "It's me," he said.

The door opened. Lamar Nichols squinted down at him. He held a Colt .45 at his side. Lamar was almost as wide as he was tall, a burly cowboy with a smoker's gravelly voice, dull brown eyes that could bore a hole through hardwood and hands large and strong enough to throttle a grown man.

"What the hell time is it?" Lamar demanded with a scowl. He wore nothing but a pair of worn jeans, his furry barrel chest bare like his feet.

"Almost two in the damned afternoon," Boone snapped. An odor wafted out of the camper. The damp small space smelled of mold, stale beer and B.O. The last thing Boone wanted was to go inside the camper with Lamar. He motioned to the weathered wooden picnic table outside next to the camper.

"Give me a minute," Lamar said and stepped back inside, closing the door.

Boone took a seat at the table facing the lake. A breeze rippled the silken green surface of the water. A few fishing boats bobbed along the edge of the red bluffs on the other side.

"So what's up?" Lamar said behind him.

Boone turned at once, never comfortable with Lamar behind him. "Clayton T. Brooks' body was found in a ravine."

"Where else would you expect a drunk has-been bull rider to end up?" Lamar said, making the picnic table groan under this weight as he sat down across from Boone. He'd put on a flannel shirt and wet down his dark hair—hair the same color as Boone's. Other than hair color, Boone had little else in common with his older half brother.

"That it?" Lamar asked rubbing a hand over his grizzly unshaven jaw, his eyes never leaving Boone's face.

"Monte's taking Devil's Tornado to the Bozeman rodeo."

Lamar nodded. "No big surprise there. He needs that bull. You've got him right where you want him." His beady eyes narrowed to slits. "What about last night?"

"I told you I'd take care of it." He didn't want Lamar going off half-cocked and ruining everything.

"You talk to Coltrane? He tell you what the hell he was doing back by Devil's Tornado's trailer?" Lamar asked.

"Said he was just curious about the bull. But he doesn't know anything." At least Boone hoped to hell that was true.

"You sure about that?" Lamar challenged. "What was he doing nosing around, then?"

Boone looked past him to the lake, his jaw tightening. "Coltrane isn't the only one interested in the bull. Everyone's curious. We just have to be careful."

Lamar cut his eyes at him. "There was someone else there last night. Someone over by the horse corrals."

Boone had hoped that Lamar hadn't seen the cowgirl.

"Coltrane tell you who the cowboy was with him?" Lamar asked.

Lamar thought it was a cowboy in the corral? Obviously he hadn't gotten a good look. Boone tried not to show his relief. Nor did he mention that asking Coltrane about the cowgirl would have been stupid.

Lamar had been told too many times in his life he was stupid. He didn't take it well anymore.

Nor was Boone going to tell his half brother that he'd tracked down the drivers of both vehicles that had been in the lot last night after Coltrane left. One led him to the Lariat Motel in Antelope Flats. The other to Asa McCall's Sundown Ranch.

"You don't think it was Monte, do you?" Lamar asked.

Boone sighed. "Trust me, it wasn't Monte."

"Yeah, well, he might think you're the greatest thing since sliced bread, but I wouldn't trust him," Lamar said picking at his ear with a thick finger. Lamar didn't trust anyone.

Boone pushed himself to his feet. "Don't worry about last night. You just take care of your end. We're going to Bozeman. Three-day rodeo. I'm thinking we might throw in a couple more bulls. See how they do."

Lamar gave him a lopsided crooked-tooth grin.

"I just want them to look promising," Boone said. "Nothing like Devil's Tornado. He's our star. But last night in Sheridan… Let's try not to let him be quite that wild, okay?"

Lamar's expression made it clear he thought Boone was making a mistake. "You're the boss."

Boone studied his half brother, hoping he didn't forget that. He didn't need to worry about keeping Lamar in line. He had other worries. Ty Coltrane. And the cowgirl who had something that belonged to him. A syringe he had to get back.

Chapter Seven

Ty Coltrane looked over at Dusty as he slowed the pickup on the outskirts of Sheridan, Wyoming.

He couldn't help worrying about her, even though he figured she was probably right. Rasmussen hadn't even seemed to notice her this morning at the ranch. He couldn't have known she was in the horse corral last night. Maybe it *had* been an accident. And maybe it hadn't been Rasmussen who'd followed her home last night.

But warning Dusty about Boone Rasmussen was still a good idea. Ty's instincts told him that Rasmussen was dangerous. And up to *something*. He just hoped to hell that it really didn't have anything to do with Dusty.

Ty parked in front of the Sheridan Boutique. Dusty shot a look at the front window and the mannequin outfitted in a skimpy cocktail dress. He could see her already digging in her heels.

"Here's the first rule," he said quickly. "You do as I say, or I take you back to the ranch right now."

She shot him a look. He could see her struggling with the need to tell him what she thought while being forced to bite her tongue.

He grinned at her. "Sit," he ordered and got out to open her door.

She scowled at him, but let him open her door. "Oh, I get it. Guys want to open your door just so they can look at your butt, huh?"

He laughed as she swayed her hips as she walked away from him. "Now you're starting to get the idea," he called as he slammed the pickup door and turned to find her waiting for him outside the shop.

Her head was tilted back, the western hat on her head no longer shading her lightly freckled face. In that instant, with the sun shining down on her, she looked like a goddess, capable of ruling the world. Certainly capable of stealing a cowboy's heart.

"Okay, let's get this over with," he said shaking off the image. "Go into that dressing room. I'll have clothes brought to you." She gave him a narrowed look. "This was your idea. You wanted my help," he reminded her as they entered the shop.

She clutched at his arm. "Promise you won't make me look silly?" she whispered. Her eyes were big and blue, as clear and sparkling as a Montana summer day.

He would have promised her anything right then. He nodded. "I promise. Now get in there."

The moment she disappeared behind the dressing

room curtain, Ty looked around for Angela. She came out of the back, smiling as she recognized him.

"Ty," she said, surprise and what sounded like pleasure in her voice. She was an attractive twenty-five-year-old, tall, slim, with big brown eyes and hair the color of an autumn leaf.

"Hi." He felt a stab of guilt. He liked Angela. They'd dated a few times. He hadn't seen much of her since then, though. He'd been busy at the ranch, but he wished now that he'd called her.

Angela was waiting, no doubt wondering what he was doing in a women's clothing shop if not there to see her.

"How long do I have to wait in here?" came Dusty's plaintive voice from the dressing room.

"Hold your horses," he called back.

Angela glanced toward the closed curtain of the dressing room, then at Ty. Her expression altered, as if it were all suddenly clear. "Your girlfriend?"

Ty hoped to hell Dusty hadn't heard that. He took Angela's arm and led her out of earshot of the dressing room. "I'm just helping out a friend. She needs everything from the ground up. Feminine stuff."

Angela nodded as Dusty stuck her head out and Ty shooed her back into the dressing room.

"It isn't what you think," he said to Angela.

She chuckled. "When a man says that, it's exactly what a woman thinks."

"Not in this case. Dusty's just a neighbor girl."

Angela nodded, clearly not buying a word of it.

"She asked me to help her. She needs some girl clothes and I haven't a clue—"

"Let's have a look at this…*girl*," Angela said, heading for the dressing room. Ty followed her as she drew back the curtain a little and stared at the fully clothed Dusty McCall and smiled, as if relieved. "Hi. I'm Angela. Let me see what I can find for you."

Dusty looked from Angela to Ty, a smug knowing glance that said she knew at once what his relationship was with the saleswoman. He closed the curtain on her look and wandered over to a rack of blouses. He found one the color of Dusty's eyes.

"What do you think about this one?" he asked Angela.

She cocked her head at him. "You have good taste. It matches her eyes." She pulled out a pair of slacks to go with the blouse. "Dresses?"

He nodded. "Nothing too…" He made a motion with his hand. "She's just a kid."

"Right," Angela said with a note of sarcasm and headed for the dress rack.

"Also, I promised her I'd help with her hair and makeup," Ty said quietly as he followed Angela to the back of the store.

She shot up an eyebrow.

"Exactly. I know nothing about either. Any suggestions?"

"Maxie next door at the beauty shop." Angela pulled

down a half-dozen dresses and looked over at him. "I suppose she will need lingerie as well."

Angela moved to the lingerie and held up a black lacy bra and panties. He nodded wondering if he looked as ill at ease as he felt. Dusty in black lace? He didn't want to think about it any more than he did the red silk teddy Angela held up. This was Slim, the girl he'd teased and tormented, trailed after and picked up from the dirt. Recently.

"Why don't you go down to the Mint Bar and have a beer," Angela suggested, seeing his discomfort. "I'll send her down when she's done." His instant relief made Angela laugh. "How did you get roped into this, anyway?"

"Like I said. She's a friend and I guess there wasn't anyone else."

Angela smiled, looking unconvinced.

"I really appreciate this," he said. "Maybe you and I could have lunch one of these days," he suggested.

"Maybe," she said, but something in her tone said there was little chance that was going to happen.

Sheepishly, he sneaked out the door as Angela headed for the dressing room and Dusty. He couldn't get out of the place fast enough and he did have some chores he could do before getting the beer.

He was too antsy to sit still, anyway. The way he figured it, if Dusty didn't kill him when she saw the clothes Angela had picked out, then Asa McCall or one of the McCall boys would for sure when they heard about this.

The good news was that Dusty wouldn't ever ask for his help again. That thought stopped him cold. He couldn't imagine not having Slim around.

He told himself that was because he'd always been around to protect her. Like a fifth older brother. And Dusty needed him around. Maybe especially now, he thought, frowning, wondering why she'd suddenly decided she needed a makeover.

LETTY WAS SURPRISED when she heard someone ring the bell in the motel office and realized she hadn't locked the door.

The No Vacancy sign was still up outside. She hadn't had time to take it down yet. The housekeepers were busy cleaning the rooms and since it was pretty early for anyone to be checking in...

If it was anyone she knew, they would have called out to her and then come on back through the narrow hallway that attached the motel office to the house.

She frowned as she stopped what she was doing—packing. Excited and anxious about the coming weekend, she'd already started packing, thinking she might camp out, as Hal Branson had suggested. In case she stayed. Sleeping bag, tent, cooler. She really needed to trade off the VW Beetle her parents had bought her for high school graduation and get herself a pickup truck.

The idea appealed to her, even though she knew it would shock her parents—that is, the Arnolds, she amended, who felt a young woman shouldn't drive a truck.

As she passed the hall mirror, she glanced at her image again. Her bright-red, long, curly, unruly hair was pulled back into a ponytail, her pale skin sprayed with reddish freckles, her eyes green, her mouth too large and filled with too many teeth.

She wondered what kind of car her birth mother drove. Would the woman look like her? Or was this the first of a long line of wild goose chases?

"There is a possibility that you were stolen from your birth mother and might never know the truth," Sheriff Cash McCall had told her when the doctor who'd done the illegal adoptions had confessed that she was one of the babies involved.

Stolen. Or maybe her mother hadn't wanted her. She couldn't help but think about Dusty's mother giving her up to Asa McCall when Dusty was a baby. Letty sighed. Maybe she and Dusty had more in common than either had known.

Letty told herself that she would tell her friend *everything* as soon as Letty herself knew the truth. But first she had to know who her birth parents were, what blood ran through her veins, what relatives she might have out there somewhere. She'd always envied Dusty her four brothers. A brother, or even a sister, would be cool.

Maybe even a mother named Flo who played in a heavy metal band. She cringed at the thought, glad Hal would be going with her to meet the woman.

The bell in the office rang again. She'd been hoping whoever it was would just go away. No such luck.

As she headed for the office, she knew part of her problem was that she'd resented the fact that her "adoptive" parents had lied to her. She'd argued with them on the phone about it recently, which only made her feel more guilty. But how had her shy, couldn't-tell-a-lie-if-her-life-depended-on-it mother managed to keep such a secret? Or, for that matter, covered up the fact that she was never really pregnant?

By isolating herself from everyone, Letty thought as the bell in the office dinged again. Her adoptive parents had been standoffish, not mixing with the community at large. Now she knew why. All to hide the biggest lie of all—Leticia herself.

As Letty came down the hallway toward the motel office, she saw the broad shoulders of a man standing with his back to the counter. He wore a gray Stetson on his dark head. Even before she saw his face, she felt a premonition quake through, just a flash of danger, fear and ultimately pain.

Boone Rasmussen turned, his dark eyes fixing on her. "Leticia Arnold?"

DUSTY STARED AT the tiny red silk bra in her hand. "You have got to be kidding." She felt like she did the first time she and Letty tried on bras. How humiliating. She'd gotten all wrapped up in the stupid thing and Letty had had to help her out of it.

Angela handed in more clothing. Dusty took it, thanked her and made sure the curtain was closed all the way before she slipped the sports bra over her head and looped the cool red silk around her, fastening it, then drawing it up over her breasts and slipping the straps over her shoulders.

The effect shocked her. She'd never owned anything but sports bras. They worked better for horseback riding.

She pulled off her boots and jeans and the same style of cotton underwear she'd worn since she was six and drew on the skimpy red silk panties. She was glad Letty wasn't here. She would have been rolling on the floor with laughter.

But the truth was, the cool red silk felt…good. Maybe too good. And she looked…okay. Better than okay. She crossed her arms over her chest, a little embarrassed. The bra made her look stacked! And the thin silk was so *revealing!*

She reached for one of the dresses and slipped it on over her head. The lightweight material dropped over her like a whisper, making her suck in her breath as she looked in the mirror.

She let out a laugh of surprise, quickly covering her mouth. That was *not* her in the mirror. No way. Well, the head was still hers, the face, the hair—but the rest…

Angela slid a couple pairs of high heels under the door and some strappy sandals.

Dusty snatched up the sandals in a pale blue that

matched the color of the dress. She slipped them onto her feet—feet that hadn't seen anything but cowboy boots since she was three. Flipping her long braid up and brushing her bangs out of her eyes, she stared at herself in the mirror. The partial transformation left her speechless.

In the mirror, she saw Angela peek through the curtain behind her. "How are you doing?"

Dusty could only nod, filled with a strange mixture of having a lump in the throat and being embarrassed.

"Stunning," Angela said and gave her a smile and thumbs up.

Dusty blushed.

"Maxie next door said to send you over and she'd show you how to do your makeup and your hair," Angela said. "This for a party?"

Dusty shook her head. "I just need a change."

Angela nodded. "Who's the guy? Never mind, I think I already know. Ty Coltrane is a lucky man." She ducked back out before Dusty could set her straight.

Dusty stood in the front of the mirror, hating to take the dress off. She tried on the others, picked three, and put the blue dress back on. "Is it all right if I wear this now?" she asked Angela when the clerk returned. She handed her the extra lingerie, the blue blouse and black slacks and two other dresses. "I'll take these, too, and the sandals. And could you box up my boots and clothing I wore in?"

Dusty took another look in the mirror, hating to admit that Ty might have been right. Maybe it *was* the clothes. She couldn't wait to get the rest of her make-over.

It surprised her, but she was anxious to see Ty's re-action. As soon as she got her makeup and hair done and figured out how to walk in these sandals. If the new her passed the Ty Coltrane test, then she would be ready for Boone. But even as she thought about it, she wondered if she would ever be ready for Boone Ras-mussen. Or if she wanted to be. Something about Boone still drew her and at the same time repelled her. If he really had opened that gate last night…

Well, she would find out for herself soon enough.

LETTY STOPPED SHORT of the motel counter as her gaze met Boone Rasmussen's dark one. She didn't like or trust him, and she feared it showed in her expression because his eyes darkened at the mere sight of her.

"Leticia Arnold?" he repeated staring at her as if try-ing to recognize her.

"Letty," she said out of habit and wished one of the motel housekeepers would come into the office. Both housekeepers were only local high school students, but Letty didn't like being alone with Boone. It was silly. She could see a housekeeper cart just two doors down. If she had to scream—

The thought shocked her. What did she think Boone would do that she would have to scream?

"Have we ever met?" he said looking around the motel office, down the hallway toward her house, then over his shoulder to the empty parking lot. Empty except for his dark green pickup.

She shook her head. "But I know who you are."

He raised a brow. "Really?"

She flushed. "If you're looking to rent a room, check-in isn't until one."

He let out a deep chuckle. "I don't want a motel room." He glanced around again, making her nervous. "I wanted to talk to you about last night. After the rodeo." He looked down the hallway again, toward her house. "Is there some place we could sit down?"

Why would Boone want to talk to *her* about last night? No way was she going to ask him into her house. "I was just going out to get some lunch." She was a terrible liar and it showed in his expression.

He flashed her a cool smile. "This late? Okay, I could use some lunch."

The last person she wanted to have lunch with was Boone Rasmussen. She'd only said that in hopes that she could cut short whatever he wanted. But clearly, he was determined to talk to her. Better at the café than here.

"We can take my truck," he said, pushing open the motel door and waiting for her. "Don't you need to get your purse?"

She hesitated, then nodded.

"Don't get me wrong," Boone said with that same

slick voice. "I'm buying. But most women I know don't go anywhere without their purses."

"I'm not like most women you know," she said without moving.

He chuckled at that. "I'll be in the truck."

This had to be about Dusty. She was doing this for her best friend.

She waited until Boone was behind the wheel of his truck before she went down the hall to her house and grabbed her small leather clutch. As she left, she locked both the house and the office. No one locked their doors in Antelope Flats. But today she was feeling strangely vulnerable.

Boone leaned across the seat as she approached the pickup and shoved open her door. With a sigh, she climbed in and closed the pickup door. *Dusty, you owe me.*

Boone looked over at her, his gaze going to her purse, his lips turning up fractionally before he started the engine.

The older model pickup was covered in mud and manure on the outside, which wasn't that out of the ordinary in a ranch town. But the inside was dirty as well, with dust, a stack of papers on the bench seat between them and empty fast-food containers on the floorboard. The cab interior smelled vaguely of onions and manure. Great combination.

"Sorry about the truck," he said as he glanced over at her again. "The hired help's been using it."

She nodded as he pulled onto the highway and drove through Antelope Flats. She'd expected him to stop at the Longhorn Café, but he drove right past it. She felt her apprehension spike before she realized where he was going. That new In and Out Drive-In outside the city limits, near the soon-to-be completed strip mall.

"Mind if we eat in the truck?" he asked as he pulled into the drive-through. "Sorry, but I don't have a lot of time. Cheeseburger, fries, cola?"

She nodded and he ordered for them both.

The radio was on low. He turned it up. "This is one of my favorites," he said of the country-and-western song playing.

She watched him tap his boot on the floor mat, the palm of his hand keeping time on the steering wheel. He's nervous, she thought. The realization made her even more apprehensive.

They were the only car in line this late. She just wished he'd get to the reason he wanted to talk to her. It certainly hadn't been for her sparkling conversational skills.

Boone took the food shoved through the window and handed her a cola, putting the sack of burgers and fries between them on the stack of papers as he paid, then drove around to the back and parked under a lone tree. They were hidden from the main road, she noted. No one would see them. Was that the idea?

He turned toward her, reached into the sack and handed her a burger and a package of fries. Her fingers trembled as she unwrapped her burger. Not that he seemed to notice. He wolfed down his burger and fries, tapping his boot to the music as if oblivious of her.

She tried to eat, but every bite seemed to grow in her mouth and didn't want to go down.

Boone finished eating and balled up his wrappers. He rolled down his window and took a three-point shot at a fifty-five-gallon barrel garbage can nearby. He missed. Letty tried to hide her smile as he swore and swung open his door, climbing out to pick it up. She bet he would have left it if she hadn't been with him.

She looked down at her food, took another tentative bite and almost jumped out of her skin when her side door suddenly swung open. She recoiled instinctively.

But Boone only moved her purse aside on the dash where she'd put it to grab some junk mail. The purse fell to the floor, spilling what little was in it. "Sorry," he said, and scooped up the contents and handed it to her before gathering up the garbage on the floorboard and taking it over to the barrel. When he slid behind the wheel again, he seemed almost too quiet.

"So what is it you want to talk to me about?" she asked. "If this is about Dusty—"

"Dusty?" he asked.

"Dusty McCall. My best friend."

He raised a brow and seemed more interested. "She was with you the other night at the rodeo?"

Finally. She knew this had to be about Dusty. She nodded. "She's the blonde with the big blue eyes. The cute one."

He nodded and rubbed the side of his jaw. "She was the one driving the pickup?" He sounded surprised by that.

"She's a ranch girl. Rides better than half the men around here. Practically ran the ranch after her dad's heart attack."

Boone smiled over at her. "Your best friend, huh?"

Letty blushed. She hadn't meant to go on so.

"So let me guess," he said glancing at her small leather clutch on the dashboard. "Dusty was the one I saw down by the corrals after the rodeo?"

She wasn't going to admit that her very smart, very capable best friend had been chasing after him. She wasn't even sure she should hint that Dusty had a crush on him. But didn't she owe her friend to at least let him know that Dusty was interested?

"She has four brothers, you know," Letty blurted out. "And they are very protective of their sister."

"I've heard of the McCall boys." Boone smiled a slow unnerving smile. "You're a little protective of her as well, it seems." His gaze shifted to her lap. "You've hardly touched your food. You seemed so anxious to have lunch when we were back at the motel."

Letty blushed again. She looked down at her lap and took a bite of her burger, knowing she'd never be able to swallow it. This had been a terrible mistake.

"I'm curious," Boone said. She could feel his eyes on her. "What exactly was your friend doing wandering around the rodeo grounds so late after the rodeo was over?"

Letty practically choked on her burger. "She was looking for you! You told her to meet you there!"

He drew back in surprise, one eyebrow going up. "Where would she get an idea like that? I don't even know her."

Letty stared at him, all kinds of smart retorts galloping through her brain. She reminded herself that her best friend had a crush on this guy. "I guess there was a misunderstanding," she said feebly. But then Letty added, "She was almost trampled by the bucking horses!"

"That corral gate has a bad latch. She was lucky," he said, the words *this time* seeming to hang in the air.

Letty felt a chill and told herself she was overreacting. What if Boone hadn't been talking to Dusty, hadn't told her to meet him, hadn't had anything to do with the latch on the gate? What if she was dead wrong about him?

"She risked her life to meet you," Letty said.

His brow shot up again and he smiled, this time the humor reaching his eyes. "I'm flattered."

Letty felt her face flame again.

He started the pickup.

She hadn't finished her burger, but he didn't seem to care as he drove her back to the motel.

"Hey," he said when she started to get out. "Why don't you give me Dusty McCall's number? If there was a misunderstanding last night, I'd like to apologize to her."

He took a pencil and a scrap of paper from the glove box and scribbled down the number Letty hesitantly gave him. "Thanks."

"Thank you for lunch," she said, good manners taking over.

As he drove off, Letty stared after him wondering what that had been about. One thing was clear. Boone Rasmussen hadn't even known Dusty McCall existed.

Well, he did now, thanks to her. Dusty was going to get her wish—a call from Boone Rasmussen.

But Letty wasn't sure she'd done her best friend a favor.

Chapter Eight

Ty was sitting in the Mint Bar drinking a cold beer, worrying about Dusty when he heard the news.

Clayton T. Brooks had been found—dead.

He took the news hard. He'd liked Clayton. "What happened?"

The bartender, a short stocky man named Eddie, told him that he'd heard that Clayton had been killed when his pickup went off the highway north of town. "He was in here Thursday night. Closed down the place, as usual."

"Do you remember him mentioning anything in particular?" Ty asked.

The bartender laughed. "Kept talking about someone named Little Joe." He shrugged. "Have no idea."

Ty nodded, remembering how Clayton had been that day at work. Now that he thought about it, he did remember Clayton mentioning Little Joe and Devil's Tornado. If only he could remember what exactly had Clayton so worked up.

"Anything specific he said about this Little Joe?" Ty asked.

The bartender shook his head. "You know Clayton. Never shut up." He smiled sheepishly. "You just tuned him out after a while. Sorry."

Ty knew exactly what the man meant. "Any idea what he was doing north of town?" There was little north of Antelope Flats, and Clayton lived in the opposite direction.

Eddie shrugged and shook his head. "No clue. Not much up that way."

Except for the Edgewood Roughstock Company ranch, Ty thought. And Devil's Tornado. Was it possible the damned fool had been going to see the bull? But who was Little Joe?

The door opened and Ty caught a whiff of perfume, something light, like a spring day, that made him turn toward the entrance for a moment.

Couldn't be Slim. She wouldn't be caught dead wearing perfume. He turned his attention back to his beer. Maybe he shouldn't have deserted her. As if his staying in the boutique would have helped matters. But he hated the thought that she might be mad at him. Might never trust him again.

He caught movement out of the corner of his eye and looked up to see a young woman moving through the series of arches along the bar's entryway. All he caught was a glimpse of her. A flash of blue and short, soft blond curls, but they were enough to hold his attention as she moved in and out of the archways. Flash. Flash. Flash. She was slim and leggy, the blue dress fluttering just above her knees as she moved. The dress the same color as the blouse he'd picked out for Dusty. The same color as Dusty's eyes.

Even when she came around the corner toward the bar, he didn't recognize her at first. True to his gender, he was looking at her curves, not her face. That is, until she stopped just feet from him.

His gaze flicked up to her face and all the breath rushed from him. "Slim?" He tried to get to his feet, practically knocking over his stool. She looked so... different. So not like the tomboy he'd known his whole life.

All he could say was, "You cut your hair!"

Her long braid was gone, her hair now chin-length, the pale blond a cap of loose curls that framed her incredible face. But that wasn't the half of the transformation. Slim had curves! He stared at her, dumbstruck.

She smiled tentatively. "So what do you think?"

When had she grown up? Sometime over the past few years and he hadn't noticed. Probably because she'd hidden it so well under those huge shirts and jackets.

He dropped back on his stool, simply flummoxed. This was Slim. The tomboy from the next ranch, the cowgirl he'd teased and tormented for years. "You're... you're gorgeous."

She cut her eyes at him as she slid onto the stool next

to him. Did she think he was kidding? She let out a long sigh, as if she'd been holding her breath. Her eyes shone. She blinked, and he realized she'd been close to tears. Did it matter that much to her what he thought?

"You aren't just saying that, are you?"

He shook his head, unable to quit staring at her. He'd wanted to help her find her girl side. He hadn't expected this kind of transformation. Asa was going to kill him. If Dusty's brothers didn't get to him first.

Eddie gave her an appreciative look, took her order and poured her a cola.

"You're okay with this new look?" Ty asked, watching her pluck up the maraschino cherry Eddie had put on top.

She leaned back her head, holding the cherry over her mouth. She was even wearing lipstick! With perfect white teeth, she nipped the cherry from its stem and took a sip of her drink, dropping the stem on her napkin.

"I feel so…different," she said and shot him a grin, the same grin that had always captivated him.

He couldn't believe this *woman* had been hidden under all that loose western clothing and that tomboy attitude. Worse, he couldn't believe she was his Slim. He felt bowled over—stunned by this change in her, of course, but even more shocked at how it made him feel.

He'd always liked her. But she'd just been a kid. The daughter of Asa McCall. The kid sister to J.T., Rourke, Cash and Brandon McCall. In other words, someone he thought of more as a buddy. A safe thought.

The thoughts he was having now weren't safe.

"Thank you for helping me," she said and took another sip of her cola.

"I think we should keep my part in this our little secret."

He caught her checking out her image in the mirror across the room. As far as he knew, the old Dusty had avoided mirrors, never seeming to care what she looked like. In a way, he missed that. He frowned, suddenly afraid he'd created a monster as she licked her lips and gave him a slow smile, as if she knew exactly the effect she was having on him.

"I can't wait to see—" she ran her finger along the top of her glass "—everyone's reaction."

Everyone? Letty, her brothers, her parents or someone else? He hated to think what effect she was going to have on young, impressionable ranch hands. He was still trying to get over the effect she was having on him.

He cut his eyes at her as a thought struck him. Was it possible she'd done this for some boy she had a crush on? He caught a gleam in her eye that he'd seen too many times before—usually when she was about to do something either dangerous or crazy, or both.

"What are you up to?" he asked, more than a little worried as he caught a whiff of the perfume he'd smelled earlier. The scent was definitely coming from Slim.

"You're scaring me," he said and meant it.

She laughed and downed the rest of her cola. The

look she shot him making it clear she wasn't going to tell him, she said, "Ready?"

He frowned at her. He wasn't ready for this new Dusty, that was for sure.

"Would you drop me off at Letty's?"

"Sure." He was relieved it was Letty she wanted to try her new look on first. That would give him time to hightail it back to his ranch before Asa McCall came looking for him with a shotgun. "Don't forget. My part in this is our little secret."

She nodded distractedly. It seemed she had already forgotten about him. The story of his life.

SHERIFF CASH MCCALL was sitting in a booth at his sister-in-law's Longhorn Café when he saw the coroner come through the door. Cash had just finished a late lunch—bacon cheeseburger, extra homemade fries and a piece of her field berry pie—when Raymond Winters slid into the booth across from him.

Cash took one look at Winters' face and said, "Whatever it is, I don't think I want to hear it."

The coroner dropped his voice and glanced around the nearly empty café. "You're going to think I'm nuts."

"I've never thought you were nuts." Raymond Winters was the most sane man Cash knew, especially considering what he did for a living.

He dropped his voice even lower. "Clayton was murdered."

Cash groaned, knowing Winters wouldn't be saying

this unless he had good reason. Cash pushed his plate away. "Okay, let's hear it."

"Well, this is where it gets crazy," Winters said. "I was examining the body and I found abrasions that could only have been made *after* Clayton was dead."

Cash frowned, trying to understand.

"There appeared to be several blows to the head that caused his death," Winters continued. "One bled profusely, but when I checked the pickup, there wasn't the type of blood splatter I would have expected to find, given that he was contained inside the pickup as it rolled. Should have been blood all over the place. Also, the head wounds aren't consistent with those from a car accident."

"You're saying he didn't die in the pickup."

Winters nodded. "But that isn't all." He looked even more upset. "I found something on the knees of his jeans and on one hand."

"What?" Cash asked, fear heavy as stones in his belly.

"Fresh bovine dung."

"I beg your pardon? Why in the hell would he have dung on him?"

Winters shook his head. "Good question. But I think you might want to order an autopsy because I'd wager my right arm that Clayton T. Brooks was murdered in some cow pasture and put in that pickup to make it look like an accident."

DUSTY COULDN'T WAIT to see Letty's face. She walked into the motel office and rang the bell rather than go right on in to her friend's attached house as she normally did.

"May I help you?" Letty asked coming out from the back.

"I'd like a room."

Letty looked up at the sound of the familiar voice, her eyes widening in shock. "Dusty?"

Dusty laughed a little embarrassed, practically crossing her fingers in the hopes that Letty wouldn't hate her new look. "What do you think?"

Letty seemed speechless. "What happened to your hair?"

"I cut it. This is the latest style. I had no idea I had naturally curly hair. What about the dress?" She turned in a slow circle and waited for Letty's reaction, a little disappointed in it so far.

"I've never seen you in a dress before."

"Because I've never had one before," she said, wishing she wasn't feeling a little annoyed by Letty's lack of enthusiasm at the change. She'd thought Letty would be as excited as she was.

"Did you do this for Boone?" Letty asked, not sounding pleased about the prospect.

"No," Dusty snapped, although she had and they both knew it. "I just decided it was time I stopped dressing like a boy."

Letty glanced down at her own clothing: jeans,

boots, western shirt. The two of them had always dressed the same.

"Not that I won't still wear my jeans and boots most of the time," Dusty added.

"You look nice," Letty said.

Nice? Dusty looked away, not wanting Letty to see how hurt she was. Part of her wanted to just turn and leave in a huff. The other wanted to say something to fix the distance she felt between them. It seemed to be widening lately, and she didn't know how to change that. "So what are you up to?"

"Nothing much."

Past her, Dusty saw what looked like a suitcase by the wall. Beside it was a cooler. A sleeping bag was rolled up on top of it. "Are you going camping?"

Letty glanced back at the suitcase. "Just putting some things away."

"Wanna grab something to eat?" Dusty asked, feeling as if she were clutching at straws.

"Already ate." Letty turned back and met her gaze. "Boone Rasmussen stopped by and took me to lunch."

Dusty couldn't hide her shock. Or avoid that sinking feeling in the pit of her stomach. "He asked you to lunch?"

"He just wanted to talk about you," Letty said quickly.

From sinking, the feeling shot to dizzying. Her stomach came alive with butterflies, her head spinning. Wasn't this what she'd wanted? "What did you tell him?"

"It was a quick lunch. He just asked your name. He saw you back by the corrals after the rodeo."

Dusty groaned. "Did he say anything else about me?"

"I'm sure you'll be hearing from him. He asked for your number. Is that lipstick you're wearing?"

Dusty nodded and fluttered her lashes. "Mascara, too."

Letty let out a long breath. "You look so…different."

"Different good, though, right?"

Her friend nodded, her smile wavering a little.

"Letty, I haven't changed."

Letty's look said she wasn't so sure about that.

ASA FOUND Shelby in the kitchen. She hadn't heard him come in. Her back was to him, ramrod straight, shoulders squared, her head up as she stood at the sink, staring out the window as if lost in thought.

She must have sensed him because she tensed, as if braced for a blow.

He stepped up behind her and, on impulse, wrapped his arms around her, burying his face into the soft sweet spot between her neck and shoulder.

She leaned back against him, a small sound escaping her throat.

He gripped her tighter, wishing he never had to let her go, needing her as he'd never needed her before and hating that even more. She deserved better. She always had.

"I love you," he whispered against her warm skin, words he had uttered too few times to her.

"Oh, Asa," she said, her voice breaking. Her body began to shake. She turned and he drew her close, cradling her head in his hands as she buried her face in his chest.

He stroked her hair, closing his eyes as he filed away the memory of its feel beneath his fingers, just as he had filed away every touch they'd shared so he would never forget.

Past her through the window he could see the warm gold cast of the sun flowing over the land. The land he'd loved so much. More than he'd loved his own wife. Fool's gold, he thought. He would give anything to turn back the clock. To undo his two most unforgivable sins. He'd chosen the ranch over Shelby, sending her away from not only him, but also from her own children.

And then he'd turned around and ransomed the ranch. Betraying his children. In the end, he'd lost what he loved most.

He smiled at the irony. His entire life had been about the ranch. Hadn't he promised his father on his deathbed that he'd make the Sundown Ranch the biggest and best? That he would do whatever it took? Sacrifice everything? Sell his very soul?

If only he could renegotiate his deal with the devil. It wouldn't be to save the ranch. It would be for those wasted years he'd spent apart from this woman in his arms. How could she ever forgive him? He'd taken her home, her life, her children. And still she loved him.

His throat closed at the thought, his chest swelling with an unbearable pain. It wasn't cancer that was eating away at his insides—it was regret.

She pulled back to look up at him, hastily wiping at her tears, as if ashamed to have broken down in front of him. Her eyes met his. He felt her stiffen, as if bracing herself. She had always known him too well.

"I'd hoped this could wait until after Cash and Molly's wedding…" He swallowed, trying not to let her hear the anguish he was feeling, failing miserably.

Her eyes filled with tears. "When do you want me to tell them all to be here?"

"Tonight," Asa said. "It's time."

Chapter Nine

By the time Dusty got home, her feet were killing her. The new bra was pinching her and the cool evening breeze had chilled her bare legs.

Letty dropped her off, declining to come in. "It's been a long day."

Her friend had told her a little more about her lunch with Boone. The important thing was that he'd not only asked about her, he'd also taken down her phone number.

Maybe he had already called, she thought as she entered the house, having forgotten about her new look—except for an unconscious eagerness to get into something more comfortable.

"What in the world?" said a familiar deep male voice from the direction of one of the chairs near the fireplace.

Dusty froze as she spotted her oldest brother, J.T., sitting in a chair by the fireplace, a stack of papers in front of him. While J.T. had married and lived on another part of the ranch with his wife Reggie, he still did most of the actual running of the ranch and spent a lot of time at the main house. She'd hoped to just sneak in without being noticed. No such luck.

"I cut my hair," she said defensively.

J.T. grimaced. "I can see that. *Why?*"

"Why not? Anyway, I like it and that's all that matters."

"That's good, because it will take a long time to grow back out."

"Who says I'm going to grow it back out?" She groaned, knowing that she'd have to go through this with all four of her brothers. J.T. was the oldest and married to Reggie. Cash, was the sheriff, and marrying Molly in a few weeks. Rourke worked the ranch with J.T. since getting out of prison and marrying Cassidy. Rourke and Cassidy had one boy and another on the way. Brandon had eloped with Anna, the daughter of the family's worst enemy.

Asa was still fit to be tied over that, since the Mc-Calls and VanHorns had been feuding for years.

"I hope you haven't forgotten that we're taking the herd up to summer pasture tomorrow morning starting at daybreak," J.T. said.

Dusty groaned under her breath. She *had* forgotten. "Of course I hadn't forgotten." No getting out of it, either. "I'll be saddled up and waiting for the rest of you before the sun comes up." She didn't give J.T. a chance to say anything else smart to her and would have stormed up the stairs to her room, but her feet were kill-ing her. She slipped off her high-heeled sandals and, carrying them, limped toward the stairs.

Behind her, she heard her brother chuckle. "Women."

Dusty smiled to herself as she topped the stairs. All her life she'd been called kid or girl. Her oldest brother had just called her a woman. That meant that this make-over had worked. Maybe Ty knew more about women than she'd thought.

Dusty tossed the sandals aside with a sigh of relief and got out of the dress and the silk underthings. With a kind of welcome-home feeling, she pulled on her cotton pants, sports bra, worn jeans and her favorite faded soft flannel shirt, one that had belonged to her brother Brandon.

Glancing in the mirror, she told herself that Letty was wrong. She hadn't changed. But when she saw her image in the glass, she knew better. Haircut aside, she now saw herself differently. She kind of missed her long hair. But there was no going back now. She had changed—and more than just her hair.

She hugged herself, remembering how she'd felt with Ty at the Mint Bar. All tingly and warm. And that was with *Ty.*

What would she feel with Boone? The thought scared her. Boone was the unknown. He was danger. Excitement. Was that why she was attracted to him? Because he was like nothing she'd never known? And only he could fulfill this desire that burned in her?

She jumped at the soft tap on her bedroom door. *"Yes?"* It had better not be J.T. to give her more grief.

Shelby opened the door and peeked in, her eyes widening at the sight of her daughter's short hair. She opened her mouth, closed it, opened it again. "We're all waiting downstairs."

Dusty blinked. "Why?"

Shelby pushed the door all the way open. "I thought one of your brothers had told you. Everyone is here for dinner. At your father's request."

Family dinners were never good news. Her brothers all had their own houses and only came to dinner at the ranch when summoned. They were all expected to attend without question.

It still irked Dusty that Shelby had come back after all those years and thought she could just step into being the mother. A mother didn't abandon her children.

"I really don't want—"

"Your father has something he wants to tell all of you," Shelby cut in, an edge to her words that brooked no argument.

"Fine. I'll be right down."

Shelby studied her for a moment, reminding Dusty of her makeover, but, to Dusty's relief, said nothing as she closed the door and left.

Dusty turned to look in the mirror. On impulse, she took off Brandon's old shirt and slipped into the blue blouse that Angela had told her Ty picked out. Amazing. As Dusty stared at herself in the mirror, she realized the blue was the same color as her eyes. Not that Ty would have realized that.

She considered putting on the slacks. Even the sandals again, but stuck with the jeans and boots. Fluffing up her short curls, she took one last look at herself in the mirror. Why tonight, of all nights, did she have to face the entire family?

But she knew that wasn't what was bothering her. The moment Shelby told her about the family dinner, worry had begun to gnaw at the pit of her stomach. For months, she'd known something was going on between her parents, ever since during one of these "family dinners" Shelby had come back from the dead.

Dusty feared that whatever her father had to tell them tonight would be even worse.

JUST OFF THE HIGHWAY, not a mile down the road toward the Edgewood Roughstock Company ranch road, Boone Rasmussen saw the big black car pulled to the side, motor running, and knew the driver had been waiting for him.

He swore as he slowed, telling himself he shouldn't have been surprised. Waylon Dobbs. He'd wondered how soon he would be hearing from the veterinarian.

Pulling his pickup behind the big shiny Lincoln, he cut the engine, leaned back and waited. If Waylon thought he was going to make this easy, he was a bigger fool than Boone had suspected.

From behind the wheel of the Lincoln, Dobbs peered into his rearview mirror. Then, seeming to realize that Boone wasn't going to come to him, he finally opened the car door and got out.

Dobbs looked nervous as hell as he walked toward Boone's pickup. Boone rolled down the window as the rodeo veterinarian came alongside and smiled as if glad to see Dobbs when he was anything but.

Waylon Dobbs was a local veterinarian who volunteered at rodeos to make sure the animals were fit. For volunteering, Dobbs got his name on one of the large signs that ringed the rodeo arena. Nothing like free publicity.

In return, Dobbs—a short, squat, bald fifty-something urban cowboy—did basically nothing, which seemed to suit him just fine—and worked well for Boone. What Dobbs didn't see didn't get him into trouble.

That was until last night's rodeo. Unfortunately, Dobbs had seen something he shouldn't have.

"I wanted to continue our discussion from last night," Dobbs said looking around nervously. He had a high, almost squeaky voice that made Boone want to strangle the life out of him. "I didn't want to take the chance that we might be overheard again."

There wasn't another soul for miles, the land spreading out in rolling hills of grass and silver sage. No one could possibly hear what they had to say, if that was what Dobbs was worried about.

"I thought we'd pretty much settled things last night," Boone said, resenting the hell out of the fact that he'd had to cut Dobbs in.

Dobbs licked at his thin lips. "It's just that I've been thinking."

Boone smiled and slowly shook his head back and forth. "That could be a mistake, Waylon." His gaze cut straight to the older man's gaze, as stark and deadly as a bullet.

Dobbs swallowed and straightened his just-out-of-the-box black Stetson. Boone wondered if the vet was already spending his take. Now that would *really* be a mistake.

"I'm risking a lot going along with this," Dobbs said, shifting from one foot to the other, his gaze traveling up and down the road for a moment before he looked at Boone again. "I have a reputation to worry about."

Boone laughed and moved so fast Dobbs never saw it coming. He swung open his pickup door, catching the vet in the chest. The force sent Dobbs windmilling backward, off balance, seemingly destined to land hard on his backside. The man's eyes were huge, his open mouth gasping like a fish thrown up on the bank.

But before Dobbs could hit the ground, Boone was out of the pickup. He grabbed the lapels of Dobbs's western-cut suit jacket and swung him around, slamming him hard against the side of the pickup.

"*Reputation?*" Boone ground out. "Let's not b.s.

each other here, Dobbs. I know why you ended up in Antelope Flats. You got run out of your practice back east. Something to do with gambling and prostitutes?"

"It was never proved," Dobbs cried. "They didn't have any evidence to—"

Boone twisted the fabric of his jacket, strangling any further denials as he leaned into Dobbs's face. "Don't underestimate my generosity," Boone said quietly. "Or my patience. That would be a mistake." He shoved Dobbs away so he could open his pickup door.

"Are you *threatening* me?" Dobbs said behind him, voice breaking.

Boone looked down at the toes of his boots and closed his eyes for a moment, then turned slowly to face him again. "Let me make this easy for you. You tell anyone what you know and I'll kill you, Waylon."

Dobbs let out a nervous laugh. "You aren't *serious*."

"Want to stake your life on that, Waylon?" Boone asked in a louder voice as he advanced on the man again.

Dobbs stumbled back, his Adam's apple bobbing up and down as he shook his head.

"So we understand each other?"

"No reason to start making threats," Dobbs said in a meek voice. "I just thought we could talk some business, that's all."

"We've talked all the business we're ever going to talk, Waylon," Boone said, feeling unusually tired.

"I understand."

"Do you, Waylon? I'd hate like hell for this to be a problem between us."

"No problem, Boone. No problem at all."

Boone studied him, afraid there was indeed a problem. One he'd have to deal with. "And you wouldn't be stupid enough to take this any further than between the two of us, would you, Waylon?"

"Just forget I even mentioned it."

"I'll try," Boone said.

Dobbs turned and practically ran back to the Lincoln.

Boone leaned against his pickup as Dobbs revved the engine and swung the car around, driving down into the shallow ditch and back up onto the road, leaving deep tracks in the dirt as he hightailed it back toward Antelope Flats.

Dust boiled up behind the Lincoln. Boone closed his eyes, fighting the dull ache behind his eyes. He couldn't trust Dobbs. Hell, the man was a walking time bomb.

With a curse, he turned and started to get into his truck when he saw something that stopped him. A second set of tracks in the ditch on the other side of the road, opposite the ones Dobbs had just made.

Boone felt something give inside him.

Waylon had turned around twice. Just now to leave. And earlier, when he'd parked to wait for yours truly.

Which meant... Boone looked up the road toward

the Edgewood Roughstock Company ranch. The stupid son of a— No, Boone told himself, Waylon wasn't stupid enough to go to Monte with this. Or was he?

JUST AS Dusty had feared, all eyes were on her as she walked into the dining room. "I cut my hair," she announced before anyone could say anything. "And I like it!" She took her chair next to her brother Rourke and looked around the table, daring any of them to give her a hard time.

"I like it, too," Shelby said.

Dusty didn't look at her mother. She didn't care if Shelby liked it or not. She took a drink from her water glass, hating that she couldn't forgive Shelby for giving her up all those years ago. It was bad enough that a mother would just turn her four young sons over to their father and leave. But to also give up her only daughter…

The rest of the women, all her brothers' wives, chimed in with complimentary things to say.

Dusty shifted her gaze to the head of the table where her father sat. She was still angry with him for the lie he and Shelby had cooked up. Not just about Shelby's alleged death. Almost twenty-two years ago, the two had met supposedly to discuss matters. The one-night "meeting" had resulted in Dusty's conception.

Later, Asa had brought Dusty back to the ranch, telling everyone he had adopted the infant after her parents had been killed.

She looked so much like her father and brothers that Dusty doubted anyone had believed that story. In fact, her brothers recently told her that they thought she was the result of an affair their father had had. They'd just never dreamed it was with their mother—not when they were putting flowers on her grave at the cemetery.

What a twisted pact her parents had made. All, according to them, because they couldn't live together and refused to get divorced. Dusty still couldn't believe the lies they'd told. Still couldn't forgive either of them. But because she'd always been her father's favorite, it was harder to continue being angry with him.

As she waited for him to comment on her new look, she realized she was holding her breath, desperately wanting his approval.

He reached for his wineglass and raised it in a salute. "You look even more like your mother."

Oh, great. As if she needed a reminder of how much she looked like Shelby.

Her father met her gaze, holding it with a tender one of his own, then looked over at Shelby in the chair to his left.

"Both the most beautiful women I have ever known," he said.

The room fell silent for a long uncomfortable moment at the intimacy of his words.

Fortunately, Martha came in to serve dinner and everyone started in at once, the men talking ranching, the women discussing drapery and wall colors since all of them except Cash and Molly had new houses. Eventually, the women began to talk about Cash's and Molly's wedding.

Dusty's new look was quickly forgotten. She breathed a sigh of relief and listened for the phone, hoping that Letty was right, that Boone would call. And that this was just a family dinner, like normal families had. Not a McCall family dinner that bode anything but well.

"So what is *this* dinner about?" her brother J.T. asked, making Dusty want to hit him. "Going to reveal another big secret?"

Silence dropped like a bucket of cold water over the room. Dusty stole a glance at her brothers. They all looked as worried as she felt, their wives just as uncomfortable and concerned.

"Getting everyone together doesn't have to be about anything," Shelby said, a little too sharply. "We're *family.*" Her voice cracked. "Can't we just eat our dinner in peace?"

No one said anything, but there were sideways glances and Dusty noticed that Shelby seemed to purposely avoid looking at Asa.

But the rest of them were looking at him. Waiting.

He cleared his throat, reached over and covered his wife's hand with his own. "J.T.'s right." She seemed to wince at his touch. Or maybe his words. Slowly she lifted her head, her lips quivering for a moment, eyes shiny.

The phone rang.

Dusty's pulse jumped. Not Boone. Not now. Not when maybe they would finally find out what was going on between her parents. The two had been acting more than weird ever since Shelby's return.

Martha appeared in the doorway. "I'm sorry to interrupt," she said quickly. "But it's the fire chief for Cash. He says it's urgent."

Cash excused himself to take the call on the phone in the hall, returning almost at once to say he had to leave. "There's been a fire at Waylon Dobbs's place tonight. He's dead. He was trapped inside. I'm sorry, but I have to go."

Shelby made a small sound, her hand going to her throat. "Cash, can't it wait for just a few—"

"Cash has to do his job," Asa said patting Shelby's hand. "It's all right. We'll do this another night. Soon."

Shelby's shoulders slumped. She dropped her head. Clearly she had hoped to finish whatever she and Asa had planned tonight.

Dusty was relieved. She'd been on an emotional roller coaster for weeks now. While she would worry and wonder, she could wait. She'd been worrying and wondering ever since Shelby had returned.

"Martha, would you serve dessert," Shelby said, surprising Dusty at how quickly her mother could compose herself.

The conversation around the table resumed with talk of Waylon Dobbs. He hadn't lived in Antelope

Flats for long and Dusty hadn't known him. She shuddered at the thought of the man being burned up in his house, though.

Her mind had gone back to niggling her about what her father had been about to announce when something her brother Rourke said caught her attention.

"He had this high-pitched and kind of squeaky voice," Rourke was saying. "Odd-looking little man. Drove a black Lincoln."

Dusty felt herself start. She'd heard that voice last night at the rodeo. That was one of the men Boone Rasmussen had been with by the horse corrals. She frowned, wondering now what they'd been arguing about.

The conversation finally came back to cattle, decorating and wedding plans, but the life felt drained out of it. Everyone seemed to be trying to act normal. As if this family could ever be normal, Dusty thought.

She picked at her dessert. Her parents had both grown exceptionally quiet, especially Shelby. What had their father been about to tell them? Dusty stared down the table at her father, hoping he would look up and that she might see the answer in his eyes. He didn't. He seemed engrossed in the chocolate tart Martha had baked—and nothing else.

But she knew better. Her heart felt heavy. She opened her mouth, desperately needing to get his attention.

He looked up, surprising her. Their eyes locked.

And she saw a pleading in his look, as if asking for her forgiveness. Her heart dropped like a stone down a bottomless well as he dragged his gaze away, the set of his jaw making it clear she would learn nothing tonight no matter how hard she pushed him.

She took a bite of her tart. Waiting for the next family dinner would be like waiting for that stone to hit bottom.

Dinner over, the women got up to help clear the dishes. Dusty hesitated, but her father didn't give her a second glance as he excused himself saying he had some business he had to attend to.

Her brothers all wandered into the living room in front of the fireplace.

The phone rang again. Shelby took it in the hall on the way to the kitchen. Dusty watched her mother's expression as she took the call.

She heard Shelby say, "Yes, Dusty is here. May I say who's calling?"

Dusty felt her pulse jump. Was it Boone?

Shelby turned to look back toward the dining room, her grave expression softening. "Oh, I'm sorry, Ty, I didn't recognize your voice. Dusty's right here. No, you didn't interrupt dinner. We'd just finished." She signaled with the phone.

Ty? Disappointment made her body heavy as Dusty put her dishes in the sink and went to take the call. She waited until her mother had returned to the kitchen before saying, "*Yes?*"

"Nice to hear your voice, too, Slim," Ty said. "Why so grumpy?"

"I'm not grumpy. There is probably a good reason you called me?"

Ty sighed on the other end of the line. "I was worried about you, okay? How did the new look go over?"

"Fine. My brothers hate it, my dad said I looked just like Shelby, then he got all teary-eyed and my mother said she loved it."

"That bad, huh?" He chuckled. "I just wanted to make sure you were okay."

"I'm okay." She glanced in the hall mirror, still surprised by what she saw, and ran a hand through her short blond curls. "Thank you for today."

"No problem."

Suddenly, she felt like crying. She told herself it was because she was worried about her father and disappointed that the call hadn't been Boone. She felt awful for being short with Ty. He'd been so good to her today. "What did you name the foal?"

"What do you think? Miracle."

She smiled. "I'm glad you called."

He chuckled, sounding almost shy. "Sure you are. You take care of yourself, okay, Slim?" He sounded worried about her, as if there was reason to be.

"Thanks," she said and hung up. Up in her room, she threw herself on the bed, feeling so overwhelmed she felt as if she were drowning. What was wrong with her?

Her private line rang. She sat up and reached for it,

quickly wiping her tears. As bad as she was feeling, she hoped it would be Letty. She really needed to talk. She snatched up the phone.

"Dusty McCall?" a male voice asked.

Her pulse roared in her ears. She swallowed the lump in her dust-dry throat. "Yes?" she managed to get out.

"It's Boone. Boone Rasmussen."

Chapter Ten

Boone sat on the edge of his bed in the bedroom Monte Edgewood had given him on the second floor at the back of the house.

Now that he had her on the line, he wasn't sure what to say. If her friend Letty was telling the truth, Dusty McCall was the one who'd been in the horse corral after the Sheridan rodeo. The one who might have overheard his argument with Waylon Dobbs. The one whom he'd seen pick up something gingerly from the dirt and put it in her bag.

The syringe he'd dropped.

He rubbed a hand over his face. "I got your number from your friend Letty?" he said tentatively. "I hope I have the right person. You were at the rodeo with your friend last night in Sheridan? I think I saw you afterward?" He thought he heard a choking sound.

"I'm Dusty McCall," a young-sounding female voice said. "I was at the rodeo last night."

Boone smiled. "Good. Then you're the one I'm looking for."

Silence.

This was going to be harder than he'd thought. What had he hoped? That she'd blurt out what she'd heard. More important, what she'd not only seen, but also now had in her possession? All day, he'd kept telling himself that maybe she didn't know what the syringe had been used for.

But it came down to only one thing: then why had she picked it up?

"Letty told me that you were almost trampled by the bucking horses when they broke through the corral gate last night," he said, trying a different approach. "I wanted to be sure you were all right."

She let out an audible sigh followed by what could have been a little laugh. "I'm fine." She sounded nervous. Or maybe she was scared. He'd tracked her down. He knew who she was.

"I'm glad to hear you're all right. I would hate for you to get hurt because of me." He waited, hoping she would say something. She didn't and he realized he was going to have to get her alone. He couldn't tell anything over the damned phone. "Letty told me you thought you were supposed to meet me after the rodeo."

A strangled sound.

"I don't think we've ever met, have we?" he asked.

"No." Definitely nervous. What did she know?

He felt his skin crawl with worry. "I apologize if

there was a misunderstanding last night. Let me make it up to you. What are you doing tonight?"

"*Tonight?*"

He glanced at the clock on the bedside table and swore under his breath. "Sorry, I didn't realize how late it was." His disappointment was real. "How about tomorrow night?"

A groan. "I'm going to be on a cattle drive with my brothers the rest of the week."

How lucky for her. And unlucky for him. Breaking into the ranch was out of the question. Far too risky. Hell, she might not even have the syringe anymore. Or it could have fallen to the bottom of her bag and she'd completely forgotten about it.

The one thing he was sure of—she hadn't given it to Ty Coltrane, or the sheriff would already be at Boone's door. "What day will you be back?"

"Friday."

Damn. "Oh, that's too bad, I'll be in Bozeman Friday night at the rodeo." A thought. "You wouldn't be planning to go to the Bozeman rodeo, would you?" Better than seeing her in Antelope Flats. If he could get her away from town, away from her family, away from Ty Coltrane.

"The Bozeman rodeo?" she echoed.

He held his breath.

"Yes, that is, I was thinking about going," she said.

Boone began to relax a little. This might work out better than he'd hoped. "Great, then it's a date."

"Great." She sounded strange.

He thought of Dobbs and hoped he didn't have another blackmailer that he would have to deal with on his hands.

"There's just one thing," he said. "I thought I saw you with Ty Coltrane last night. If the two of you are… involved…"

He heard a gasp on the other end of the line. "No! We've just known each other since we were kids."

"You're not…seeing him then?"

"*No.*"

"My mistake. I thought I saw you together last night."

Another strangled sound. "We ran into each other after the rodeo."

With a silent groan, Boone lay back against the headboard and closed his eyes. There was no way he'd told this Dusty McCall chick to meet him after the rodeo. Then on top of that, Ty Coltrane had been sneaking around Devil's Tornado and then he and Dusty had just happened to hook up.

At least Coltrane had been honest about the fact that he'd been there prying into Boone's business.

What did Dusty McCall want? If she'd given the syringe to anyone, wouldn't they have taken it to the rodeo veterinarian? And Waylon Dobbs would have told Boone today on the road. Dobbs would have used it as leverage for more money to keep his mouth shut.

Boone had feared that Waylon had driven down to

the Edgewood Ranch house today, maybe told Monte what he knew, hoping to get even more money.

But fortunately Monte had been the same old Monte, clasping him on the shoulder, calling him son, offering him a cold beer, which meant his only loose end now was Dusty McCall. She either still had the syringe. Or, if he had any luck at all, would have discarded it by now, not realizing what she had in her hot little hands.

Either way, Boone would find out in Bozeman. It was the being patient part that was hard. He couldn't chance the syringe getting into the wrong hands.

"So I guess I'll see you Friday night," he said, trying to keep the frustration out of his voice. "Look me up when you get to the rodeo and we can make plans for later."

"Okay."

"Good. I'm really looking forward to this." He hung up and swore. Dusty McCall was the last thing he needed.

DUSTY HUNG UP and mentally smacked herself for being so tongue-tied on the phone with Boone. She sat for a moment, too stunned to move. Boone had asked her out. Wasn't that what she'd been hoping for?

She picked up the phone and called her best friend.

"Boone called. He asked me out," she blurted, surprised that she was half hoping Letty would try to talk her out of it.

"I figured he would." Letty didn't sound all that happy about it, but didn't put up an argument.

"We're going out Friday after the rodeo in Bozeman. Go with me. Please."

"I can't," Letty said.

"Go. I promise I'll make it up to you. I need you with me," Dusty pleaded.

"I can't. Really. There's something I have to do next weekend."

"Oh."

"I'll tell you about it as soon as I can," Letty said.

Dusty rolled her eyes, pretending it didn't hurt. But it did. "If there is something I've done—"

"No. It's not like that. It's just something I have to take care of."

Sure. Dusty couldn't believe this. "Okay." She bit back a snotty reply, telling herself that Letty was obviously going through something, something big, something she didn't want to share. Dusty wondered if it could have anything to do with part of an argument she'd overheard between Letty and her elderly parents who lived in Arizona.

Whatever it was, Letty hadn't confided in her and that hurt more than she could bear. Letty had been her best friend since grade school and they'd never kept secrets from each other. Until now.

"Well, I guess I'll talk to you when I get back then." She hung up, feeling even more apprehensive about her date with Boone and sick inside over Letty. She was losing her best friend.

SMOKE DRIFTED UP from the blackened shell of what was left of Waylon Dobbs's house. A few firemen moved around in the debris, putting out spot fires.

Cash parked his patrol car behind the coroner's van and got out. The acrid air burned his throat and eyes as he walked toward where Coroner Raymond Winters stood leaning against a fire truck.

Winters took a drink from a can of root beer, tipping the can at Cash in greeting. "We have to quit meeting like this. You know Waylon?"

"Just to say hello. How about you?"

The coroner shook his head. "This used to be the old Hamilton place. I always liked this house. No other houses close by."

"Morgan know what happened?" Cash asked.

Winters peered at him over the top of his root beer can, but said nothing as he took a drink. Cash was beginning to know the look only too well. Past Winters, Cash saw Fire Chief Jimmy Morgan head his way, face covered in soot, expression grim.

The Antelope Flats Fire Department, like those in a lot of rural towns in Montana, was made up of volunteers, except for the chief and assistant chief.

Morgan pulled off a glove and mopped a hand over his face. "Started at the back of the house. Some kind of accelerant was used. Place went up like a torch."

Cash frowned. "Arson?"

"Won't have a definite on that until the investigators

get here from Billings," Morgan said. "For my money? Arson."

"Fire started at the back of the house?" Cash asked, not liking what he was thinking. "It was too early for Waylon to be sleeping. He would have had time to get out."

"Don't see why not," Morgan said. "There would have been a rush of noise when this baby was set and lots of smoke. No way he could have missed it unless he was passed out."

"Or already dead," Winters said.

Cash shot him a look.

Winters shrugged. "Just a thought."

"Is it possible Waylon started the fire?" Cash asked Morgan.

The fire chief looked doubtful. "Suicide?" He pulled his glove back on slowly, studying it as if thinking about that possibility before he spoke. "I suppose it's possible. Found the body in the first-floor bedroom. On the bed."

"That's not suicide, that's just plain crazy," Winters said. "Start the fire, take off to the bedroom and wait to burn to death?"

"He probably would have died of smoke inhalation before the fire reached him," Morgan said.

It sounded as implausible as hell. But otherwise, why wouldn't Waylon get out? Unless Winters was right and Waylon had already been dead.

"The neighbor up the road there called it in." Morgan pointed a few blocks away. "Remember Miss Rose?" Now retired, she'd taught first grade to most of them. "I'll send you a copy of my report, along with the state fire inspector's. He's on his way from Billings."

One of Morgan's men called to him. He excused himself and went back toward the house.

"We'll need an autopsy," Cash told Winters.

Winters nodded. "I know you're hoping for accidental death here. Or if not, suicide. But if the fire really was arson, then we gotta wonder if we don't have another suspicious death on our hands."

Cash was thinking the same thing. "I'm going to talk to Miss Rose and see if she saw anything, since hers and Waylon's were the only two houses on this road. Go ahead and move the body. Morgan will have photographed everything for his report." First Clayton. Now Waylon.

He walked the few blocks to Miss Rose's house and knocked. Rose Zimmer answered immediately. Clearly she'd been expecting him.

"Hello, Cash," she said in that tone he remembered too well from first grade. Instantly, he felt like her student again.

"I just need to ask you a few questions about the fire."

She had to be eighty if she was a day, but she didn't look it. She motioned him in with an impatient flick of her wrist.

He wiped his feet on the mat and stepped in. Before

he could even ask, she succinctly told him what she had witnessed, explaining that she had smelled smoke, gone to the window, seen flames coming from the roof of Waylon Dobbs's house and dialed 911.

Cash jotted it all down in his notebook, taking care not to let her see his penmanship. "Did you see anyone near the house?"

"Not at the time," Rose said. "But after the call, I looked out and saw a dark-colored pickup go by. I'm sorry I didn't get a license plate number for you. It was too muddy. Didn't recognize it or the driver. Too much glare off the windshield with the sunset."

Cash thanked her, not surprised by her thoroughness. The problem was that ninety-percent of the county drove dark-colored pickups.

"He was inside, wasn't he," she said.

"I'm afraid so."

"I saw him come home earlier." She gave a small shake of her head, lips pursed. "He was driving so fast, kicking up way too much dust. I wondered what his big hurry was."

Cash wondered, too. "And he didn't leave again?"

She shook her head.

"Did you know him very well?"

"No one did," she said without having to think about it. "Stayed to himself. I'd see his light on late at night and the flicker of the television screen. I don't think he was much of a reader." Disapproval tainted her tone.

Cash closed his notebook and put it back into his

pocket. "Well, thanks again. If you think of anything else, would you please call me?"

She clucked her tongue. "I think you know me well enough, Cash McCall, that you don't have to ask me that."

He smiled. "Good night, Miss Rose."

"Good night, Cash."

As Cash started back toward his patrol car, he saw Ty Coltrane pull in and get out of his pickup.

TY HAD BEEN IN TOWN when he'd heard the fire trucks and seen the smoke. But it was a disturbing rumor that brought him to Waylon Dobbs's place to look for the sheriff.

"Ty," Cash said as he approached.

"Got a minute, Cash?"

"Sure." He motioned toward his patrol car. Ty climbed in as Cash slid behind the wheel. "What's up?" the sheriff asked.

"I just heard that Clayton was murdered. Is that true?"

"I should have known the moment I started asking questions around town, it would hit the grapevine," Cash said with a shake of his head. "Let's just say his death is under investigation."

Ty pulled off his straw hat and raked his fingers through his hair. "I don't know if this has anything to do with anything."

"If you know something Ty, I'd like to hear it."

He shoved the hat back on his head and looked at Cash again. "The day he died, Clayton was all worked up over a bull. I know," Ty hurried on, "Clayton was always worked up over some bull or another, but this bull was Devil's Tornado. I'm wondering if Clayton didn't go out to the Edgewood Roughstock Company ranch the night he died to have another look at the bull."

"This bull, it's one of Monte's?" Cash asked.

Ty shook his head. "No, it's Boone Rasmussen's. I saw the bull perform at the Sheridan, Wyoming, rodeo and I got to tell you, it was acting pretty strange."

"Strange how?" Cash asked.

"Like maybe it had been drugged," Ty said, the words finally out.

"*Drugged?* I don't know anything about rodeo, but is that possible?"

"I've never *heard* of anyone drugging roughstock," Ty agreed. "But I think it's possible. This bull seemed disoriented, confused, I don't know, high on something, something that made it buck like a son of a gun."

"Let's say you're right. Wouldn't the rodeo veterinarian have noticed?"

"Not necessarily. Rodeo vets are volunteers and usually only concerned if an animal appears sick or hurt, or falls down three times in the arena," Ty said.

"So you don't know if the volunteer veterinarian noticed anything unusual about Devil's Tornado at the Sheridan rodeo," Cash said.

"No."

Cash pulled out his notebook. "Well, there is one way to find out. Do you know who the veterinarian was?"

"Waylon Dobbs."

Ty looked toward what was left of Waylon's house. "Is he…?"

"Dead," Cash said.

Ty sighed and shook his head. "Maybe it's nothing, but last night after the rodeo in Sheridan, I heard Waylon arguing with Boone Rasmussen and that cowboy who works for him, Lamar."

"Did you happen to hear what they were arguing over?" Cash asked.

"No. But I'm wondering if Waylon hadn't noticed the same thing I did about the way Devil's Tornado was acting and confronted Boone about it," Ty said.

Cash was wondering the same thing.

BOONE HAD JUST hung up the phone when he heard the soft click of his bedroom door opening. He looked up from where he sat on the bed. The room Monte had given him was in a small addition off the back on the second floor—fortunately not within hearing distance of the master bedroom Monte shared with his young bride downstairs at the front of the house.

Sierra slipped in, closing the door behind her. She wore a thin white gown that seemed to shimmer in the pale light from the lamp beside Boone's bed. She'd come straight from the shower. Her blond hair was wet and dark against her skin. She smelled of the French soap she liked. Her feet were bare.

He swung his boots up on the bed, stretching out, hands behind his head on the pillow as he watched her, pretending that this didn't scare the hell out of him.

She hadn't moved from just inside the door. Nor had she said a word. She just stood there, looking at him.

It wouldn't take much to send her away. A word. Even a look. He hated that he wanted her. And she knew it.

With a curse, he reached over and turned out the lamp. He could still see her in the faint light that bled through the thin curtains as she walked over to the side of the bed.

He closed his eyes. The bed squeaked softly as she curled up next to him. He felt her fingers in his hair, then her lips at his temple, her breath skittering over his skin.

It wasn't too late to send her away.

"Your shirt smells like smoke," she whispered, pulling back a little.

"Lamar's been smoking in my pickup again." He grabbed her shoulders, shoving her down on the bed as he rolled over on top of her, jerking the flimsy gown up as he unzipped his jeans and took her, driving himself into her again and again. The only sound was the squeak of the bedsprings and his own ragged breath until he finally found release.

Spent, he rolled off and sat on the side of the bed,

his back to her. But not before he'd seen her smile up at him. A knowing smile that said she owned him.

He heard the bedsprings squeak once more as she got up and left, closing the door quietly behind her, leaving behind not only her scent on his skin, but also the memory of her still in his blood. He rushed into the bathroom, dropped to his knees and threw up in the toilet, just as he'd done all the other times she'd come to him.

Chapter Eleven

Boone woke up hung over. He opened one eye a crack. Daylight bled through the thin curtains, the sky outside a pale pink.

Monte was sending him to Texas for a few days to look at some bulls. Boone couldn't shake the feeling that he just wanted to get him out of town. Otherwise why trust him with something this important?

According to Monte, everyone in town was in an uproar because the sheriff was asking a lot of questions about Clayton T. Brooks's death. Rumor had it that Clayton had been murdered.

Boone tried to sit up, but fell back sick to his stomach. He had to catch a late morning flight out of Billings, which meant he had a three-hour drive ahead of him, so he had to get up.

He started to close his eyes, desperately needing more sleep. But he couldn't chance missing the flight.

Lifting his left arm, he squinted at his wristwatch. Maybe he could get in a few more minutes.

Both eyes flew open. Only a white strip shone on his wrist where the watch had been. He sat up, head reeling from the sudden movement. Swiveling around, he looked to the small table beside the bed, trying not to panic.

Monte had bought him the watch after Devil's Tornado's first rodeo. He couldn't have lost it.

But the watch wasn't on the table—just the empty bourbon bottle. He had hit the bourbon hard after Sierra left last night and must have passed out.

Getting up, he searched the small room, finally dropping to his knees to look under the bed.

No watch.

Awkwardly, he got to his feet, his heart beating abnormally fast, his pulse a deafening drum. He gripped his head in both hands, telling himself it was just a watch. Hell, would he really want to keep it when this was over? He could buy his own watch one day. An even more expensive one.

But he knew that wasn't the problem.

He plopped down on the foot of the bed and scrubbed at his face with his hands as he tried to remember the last time he'd seen it. Did he have it on yesterday when he'd stopped to talk to Waylon? He couldn't remember.

It was one thing to lose the watch. It was another to worry about where it would turn up.

Monte had had Boone's damn initials engraved on it.

SHERIFF CASH MCCALL was disappointed when he called Monte Edgewood to find that Boone Rasmussen had flown to Texas and wouldn't be back until Thursday.

But he told Monte he still would drive out; he had a few questions for him. Monte had seemed surprised, but said he would be there.

True to his word, Monte was waiting on the porch. He walked toward the patrol car as Cash parked.

"Howdy, Sheriff." He extended his hand.

Cash had known Monte his whole life. After years of riding saddle broncs, Monte had started the Edgewood Roughstock Company. Cash did a little research and found out that while Monte wasn't one of the top roughstock producers in the country, he was definitely getting a name for himself. Especially in the past six months, when he'd hooked up with Boone Rasmussen and his bulls. The name Cash kept hearing was: Devil's Tornado.

"What can I do for you?" Monte asked. "I get the impression this isn't a social call."

"I need to ask you some questions about Clayton T. Brooks's murder."

Monte drew back in surprise. "Clayton's *murder?* I thought he was killed in an automobile accident."

"It appears his killer just wanted us to believe that," Cash said.

Monte frowned as he rubbed a hand over his jaw. "Clayton murdered. I can't believe it."

"The day Clayton died, all he'd been talking about

that day was one of your bulls, Devil's Tornado," Cash said. "It seems Clayton saw the bull at the Billings rodeo."

"Yeah, Devil's Tornado was in rare form that night in Billings, that's for sure," Monte said. "But what does that have to do with Clayton's...death?"

"Maybe nothing. It sounds like your bull is causing quite a *lot* of talk," Cash said. "I understand the more talk, the more money's he's worth."

Monte smiled and nodded. "But you know he's not my bull. He's Boone's. I'm helping him out by using some of his bulls. As it turns out, Devil's Tornado is helping us both."

"What is Boone doing in Texas?" Cash asked.

"Checking out some more bulls for us. He has a good eye. His father was in the roughstock business, you know."

Cash knew. He'd been learning more about rodeo and roughstock than he'd ever wanted to. "When will Boone be back?"

"He's flying in to Billings Friday morning but going straight to Bozeman for a three-day rodeo we're putting on there." Monte seemed to hesitate. "Boone didn't have anything to do with Clayton's death. I've known Boone since he was a boy. He's had his share of troubles, but he's trying to turn his life around."

Cash wanted to warn Monte about Boone. He'd learned a lot about rodeo roughstock—and Boone Rasmussen. Boone had been in trouble since he was fifteen. Nothing that had him behind bars for more than a few months, but the pattern was there.

"As for Devil's Tornado…" Monte pointed toward a bull standing alone in a small pasture. "That's him *right* there."

Cash shaded his eyes, squinting as he walked to the pasture fence, surprised at how ordinary the bull looked. "He's not what I expected."

"Doesn't look like much, does he?" Monte chuckled as he joined him. "But put him in a chute and look out. I've never seen a bull like him. He just keeps coming up with new tricks to throw riders."

"Is there any chance Clayton came out to the ranch the night he died?" Cash asked. "That would have been Thursday, probably after the bars closed."

Monte looked surprised. "Why would Clayton come out here?"

"I don't know. Maybe to see Devil's Tornado."

"We had the bull in the pasture down there." Monte pointed up the road. "But I would have heard a vehicle drive in. Even if it was late. I'm a light sleeper."

"Monte, I'm going to need a sample of Devil's Tornado blood."

Monte drew back. "His blood? You're serious."

Cash studied the docile bull in the pasture. "If I have to, I can get a warrant."

Monte shook his head and gave him a smile weighted with sadness. "That won't be necessary, Cash. I have a contract with Boone to use the bull for rodeos. I can okay any tests you need to run. Especially if it will help you find Clayton's killer. It just upsets me to think that your investigation has led you here."

ALL BOONE WANTED WAS a good night's sleep. But when he parked his pickup in front of the Edgewood house after the long flight from Texas and then the three-hour drive home, he saw that a light was on in the kitchen.

He'd changed his flight at Monte's request so he could come back early rather than meet Monte in Bozeman. Boone was worried about his damned watch, worried about leaving Lamar alone for too long, worried about Dusty McCall and the syringe, just plain worried and anxious.

"Boone, son, could you come in here?" Monte said, the moment Boone stepped inside the house.

Something in Monte's tone warned him. Boone tried to keep his cool as he stepped into the kitchen.

Monte sat at the table alone, a bottle of beer in front of him, several empties off to the side. He'd been there for a while.

The older man looked up and Boone saw at once that whatever had kept Monte up so late wasn't good.

"The trip went really well," Boone said filling in the silence. "I found a couple of bulls that would be great additions to your herd. I'll tell you all about them in the morning. I'm really beat."

"Have a seat, son," Monte said as if he hadn't heard.

Boone stood for a moment, then pulled out a chair.

He wondered where Sierra was and how worried he should be.

"The sheriff stopped out while you were gone," Monte said and took a drink of his beer.

Boone held his breath and waited.

"He seems to think Clayton was murdered and that he came out here the night he was killed to look at Devil's Tornado."

Boone tried to show the right amount of surprise and sorrow. He'd never gotten it right. "Why would Clayton be interested in our bull?"

Monte smiled slowly at *our bull,* but the smile fell short of his eyes. "There anything you want to tell me, son?"

Boone gave that some thought, pretty sure Monte was asking about a lot more than just Clayton. What would Monte do if he told him the truth? "I don't know what you want me to say."

Monte seemed disappointed by that answer. Or was it relief? "Cash is going to want to talk to you."

Boone nodded, pretending that didn't worry him. He hated the law and unfortunately had had more than his share of run-ins with police in the past.

"It troubles me that the sheriff's investigation led him to my door," Monte said and took another drink.

Boone could only nod, his mind racing. "I guess you won't want to use Devil's Tornado at the Bozeman rodeo, then."

"Cash had the lab come out and take some blood

from the bull," Monte said picking at the label on his almost empty beer bottle. "The sheriff had it in his head that the bull might have been drugged."

Boone couldn't breathe, even if he had dared to take a breath.

"But when I talked to him yesterday, he said he didn't find any drugs." Monte looked up. "Where would he get a fool idea that we were drugging Devil's Tornado?"

Boone forced himself to take a breath. "I'm just glad the sheriff knows there was no truth to it."

Monte nodded, even smiled a little. "You ought to get to bed. You look like you've been rode hard and put to bed wet. We're taking Devil's Tornado to the Bozeman rodeo tomorrow. We'd be fools to pull the bull now, don't you think? He's a star in the making."

Boone got to his feet. Every instinct in him told him to hit the road and not look back. With the sheriff sniffing around asking questions about that damned dead bull rider and Ty Coltrane snooping around Devil's Tornado, the safest thing he could do was sell his bulls to Monte, cut his losses and move on. There would always be other bulls. Unfortunately, there were few marks as easy as Monte Edgewood.

"I suppose you heard the other news," Monte said as Boone started toward the door. "Someone set a fire at Waylon Dobbs's place the night before you left for Texas. Burned to the ground. Poor Dobbs. I guess he couldn't get out."

"That's too bad," Boone managed to say as he glanced back at Monte.

Without getting up, Monte reached into the fridge and snared another bottle of beer from the door. "'Night, son," Monte said and snapped open the twist-off with his huge paw of a hand.

Boone went upstairs to his bedroom. That night, after everyone was asleep, he told himself he could get up and leave. But he knew he wouldn't. He'd come this far, risked so much; he'd be a fool not to see this through.

If he had to, he'd sell Devil's Tornado and the other bulls after the Bozeman rodeo and leave town.

By then, he would have taken care of the only other loose end he had to worry about now—Dusty McCall. He could only hope that she'd discarded the syringe days ago. But if there was a chance she'd held on to it for any reason…

Tonight, he locked his bedroom door. He thought he heard the soft rattle of the knob sometime during the night, but maybe he'd just imagined it.

Bozeman Rodeo Grounds

TY COLTRANE TOLD HIMSELF he had no business in Bozeman. He had a horse ranch to run. But the talk around Antelope Flats was that Clayton T. Brooks had been murdered—and possibly Waylon Dobbs as well.

First, an old bull rider who had been upset about Devil's Tornado had been found dead on the highway north of town, just miles from the Edgewood Rough-stock Company ranch. Then Waylon Dobbs, the veterinarian that Ty had seen arguing with Boone Rasmussen after the rodeo not a week ago had been killed in a fire.

Both tied to Rasmussen.

Cash had called yesterday to say that the blood sample on Devil's Tornado showed no sign of drugs and while he was still investigating both Clayton's and Waylon's deaths, he had nothing that tied either to Rasmussen.

Ty had been so sure Devil's Tornado had been drugged the night of the rodeo in Sheridan. He'd been around livestock his whole life. He knew when an animal was acting strangely. How could he have been that wrong?

He shook his head.

But Ty knew he hadn't driven five hours because of Boone Rasmussen—or Devil's Tornado. No, he thought, as he parked at the back of the rodeo lot and got out. He wasn't here because of some bull or some roughstock producer. He was here because of Dusty.

And he was late. The rodeo was almost over.

But the truth was: he hadn't been able to get her off his mind. Not the cowgirl who'd peeked over the stall door to watch the birth of the foal, nor the one who'd come into the Mint in that blue dress.

This afternoon when he'd called the McCall ranch and found out that Dusty had gone to Bozeman to the rodeo, he'd had the craziest feeling that she needed him.

Yeah, right.

But hey, look what had happened to her at the last rodeo. She'd almost been trampled by a herd of bucking horses. Then someone had followed her home. There was true cause for concern when it came to her.

And now she'd driven five hours to go to a rodeo in Bozeman? And without Letty, according to Shelby. What was up with that? Dusty and Letty had been attached at the hip since grade school.

As he started toward the rodeo arena, he spotted the Sundown Ranch pickup that Dusty drove. He'd never believed in premonitions, but he couldn't shake the feeling that she was in trouble.

Or maybe that was just an excuse to see her.

Either way, once inside, he scanned the grandstands for Dusty's adorable face, warning himself that she wasn't going to be happy to see him.

LETTY KNEW the moment she saw the man standing in the shade at the entrance to the rock concert that he was Hal Branson. She smiled to herself as she watched him try to smooth down the cowlick in his carrot-orange hair.

Her heart did a little flip inside her chest. She knew it was silly, but the fact that he had red hair struck her as fortuitous.

He wore new jeans and a button-down blue checked shirt. She couldn't help smiling as she neared him, betting with herself whether his eyes would be blue or brown. Blue, she decided.

He spotted her and straightened, his smile tentative. "Leticia?" His gaze went to her hair and she saw his expression almost relax.

She touched her wild mane of red hair, a shade darker than his own. "It seems we have something in common," she said and gave him a shy smile, even though she'd always been self-conscious about her teeth.

His smile broadened, lighting up his blue eyes. Up close she could see a sprinkling of freckles across his nose and cheeks. She knew without having to ask that he'd hated them since kindergarten, just as she had hated hers.

He seemed to study her, his jaw dropping slightly, his eyes wide and intent. He was about her age, maybe a few years older. Her heart beat a little faster and her face flushed warm under his perusal.

He cleared his throat. "Sorry. I didn't mean to stare. It's just…"

She'd only talked to him a couple of times on the phone, but both times she'd liked his voice. It was soft and reassuring.

He was still staring. "We could be twins. We're not," he added quickly. "Related, that is."

She laughed nervously. "I'm glad to hear that."

His eyes locked with hers. He swallowed, as if he had a lump in his throat. "You're probably going to think I'm crazy but do you believe in…fate?"

She smiled, forgetting that she'd always felt her teeth were too big for her mouth. "I'm beginning to."

TY WONDERED IF he would ever find Dusty. The grand-stands were full. A truck circled the dirt oval dragging a rake as a team prepared the arena for the next event. Loud country music played over the outdoor speakers and a clown told jokes to the crowd.

He caught sight of Lamar by one of Monte Edge-wood's semitrucks and trailers. A few cowboys hung around the empty chutes talking. He wondered if he'd get to see Devil's Tornado tonight. No sign of Rasmussen.

And no Dusty.

At least, not in the stands. Maybe she was at one of the concession stands.

He turned. His heart did a two-step at the sight of her coming toward him. She smiled and waved, and all he could do was stare.

She was dressed in jeans, ones that fit like a glove, and a sleeveless halter top that hugged her curves.

All these years, he'd liked her. But at that moment, he finally admitted it had been a whole lot more than that. He couldn't keep kidding himself. He was wild about her, and always had been.

He stopped walking, frozen in midstep, his breath seizing in his chest as the simple truth of it staggered him.

She was still coming toward him, her grin turning into a dazzling smile as she got closer. She looked a little shy, a little unsure. He knew *that* feeling! He couldn't move. Couldn't speak.

He wasn't sure when he realized that she wasn't looking at *him*, but at someone over his right shoulder.

He glanced back and in that instant, saw whom she was headed for—Boone Rasmussen.

It came to him in a blinding flash. The smile. The wave. The gleam in her blue eyes. The *new* look.

It had all been about *Boone Rasmussen!*

No! Anyone but Rasmussen.

Dusty didn't even seem to notice Ty as she walked right past. Her eyes were only on Rasmussen. And from the way he was looking back at her…

Ty let out a curse. He had to be mistaken. But even before he turned to watch her with Boone, he knew he wasn't.

Dusty shifted one hip and cocked her head, the soft blond curls swaying a little as she leaned toward Rasmussen grinning that devilish grin of hers, blue eyes wide. No mistake. She was flirting! And to make matters worse, Rasmussen was responding. But then, what man wouldn't?

Ty let out another curse. When had this all happened? He frowned as he remembered the morning at his ranch. Rasmussen hadn't even noticed the old Dusty. So why the interest now?

Could it simply be because that Dusty had looked like a cow*boy?* Because this one looked like what she really was: a very desirable woman? Mentally he kicked himself. Slim had been transformed. And what fool had helped with this makeover?

Ty groaned. Or could there be more to Rasmussen's interest in Dusty? Did this go back to the night after the Sheridan rodeo?

He swore. He'd tried to warn Dusty off Rasmussen, but in retrospect he realized that would only have made her more curious about the cowboy. Ty could only blame himself that Dusty was now a Scud Missile— and headed right for Boone Rasmussen. Right for a man that Ty believed capable of anything. Even murder.

Chapter Twelve

It took every ounce of Ty's restraint to keep him from going after Dusty.

All he could do was stand back and watch as Rasmussen ran a finger down Dusty's arm to her hand clutching the top of her leather shoulder bag. Dusty was nervous, something Ty noticed because he knew her so well. What the hell did she think she was doing?

The rodeo announcer called for the last event: bull riding. Rasmussen leaned toward Dusty, whispered something in her ear. Ty swore, desperately wanting to slug the guy.

As she swung around, Ty saw her face. It was flushed. She headed right for him but he could tell she hadn't seen him yet.

He swore under his breath and tried to go back to thinking of her as just the kid next door.

No chance of that.

"Slim," he said as she approached. It didn't matter that the nickname no longer fit her. She was still his

Slim. Past her, he saw that Rasmussen had stopped to look back.

"Ty? What are you doing here?" She looked more than surprised. She looked worried. "You're going to mess up everything." She started to walk past him.

"Oh, no you don't," he said grabbing her arm before she could get away. "You and I need to talk."

THE TRIPLE-X-FILES were just coming on stage when Letty and Hal reached the bandstand.

Letty quickly scanned the band members. They were all at least in their fifties, all hippies with long hair, a lot of it gray, wearing ragged shirts and worn jeans. But they appeared to be the real thing, and she found something about that endearing.

There was no sign of Flo Hubbard.

The band broke into a rock introduction and a tall woman with flaming red hair streaked with gray came bounding onto the stage, strumming a guitar. She wore a cutoff western shirt and worn jeans that hugged her slim body. She was barefoot, her toenails painted a rainbow of colors.

Her head was down so all Letty saw at first were her hands—hands that were so much like her own she felt tears burn her eyes. Her heart began to pound louder than the music.

The woman raised her head.

Letty's chest swelled, filling as if with helium. Her joy spilled out in tears. She felt Hal take her hand and squeeze it. She squeezed back, choking on the sobs that rose in her throat.

All those years of desperately needing someone who looked like her. Letty stared at the woman on stage, the face and green eyes so like her own, and felt as if she'd finally come home.

She'd found her birth mother.

BOONE WATCHED Coltrane draw Dusty McCall around the corner of the grandstands, their heads together conspiratorially. Something definitely going on between them. Dusty had lied about how close she and Coltrane were. He could see that just looking at the two of them together.

Why did that surprise him? Just moments ago, she'd been flirting with him. Teasing him. She had the syringe. Of course she did. He recalled now the way she'd had her hand over the top of her shoulder bag.

Women, they were all alike. Hadn't he learned that from his mother, who'd run off and left him with that low-life father of his?

He swore and turned to go back to find out what was going on with little Miss Dusty McCall. Sierra Edgewood stepped in front of him.

"Going somewhere?" she asked as she caressed the collar on his shirt.

He stepped back just out of her reach. Speaking of women… "I don't have time for this right now," he said impatiently. Was the woman crazy? Monte was over by the chutes. He could be watching them at this very moment.

She lifted one finely sculpted brow. "Maybe you'd better *make* time."

Something in her tone brought his attention away from the spot where Coltrane and Dusty had disappeared.

Sierra smiled, but something was different about her. "Now you're listening. That's more like it." She was looking at him as if she knew something. No, as if she had something on him. Even more leverage than just his inability to turn her away from his bed?

"Is this about my watch?"

She frowned. "Your watch?"

"Never mind," he said seeing her confusion. "What is it you want?" He hated being cornered.

"I missed you last night," she said with a nervous laugh.

So she *had* tried his door. He glanced toward the chutes, saw Monte watching them. Monte motioned to him. "I've got to get to work."

"Tonight after the rodeo. And Boone, don't disappoint me." She turned and walked off before he could answer.

Boone looked toward the chutes and saw Monte's eyes following Sierra, the look on his face twisting Boone's insides. Monte loved his wife, trusted her. Trusted everyone. Even Boone Rasmussen. Maybe especially him.

When Boone glanced back toward the grandstands where Coltrane and Dusty had gone, he swore. He should be helping Monte and Lamar with the bull riding. But he had to find out what Coltrane and little Miss McCall were up to first.

CASH AND HIS soon-to-be wife Molly had just finished dinner when State Fire Inspector Jim Ross called.

"Sheriff? I've got the final report on the Waylon Dobbs fire. There's something you need to see."

Cash drove over to what was left of the Dobbs place. Ross was waiting for him in his Chevy Suburban and motioned Cash inside.

"You already know that the fire was intentionally set at the back of the house. It appears the arsonist entered through a window and made his exit through the same window. We found this caught on a nail of the window frame." Ross lifted an evidence bag.

Cash's pulse jumped at the sight of a watch inside. The leather band, now partially burned, appeared to have broken prior to the fire.

Ross nodded. "It gets even better. The back of the watch is engraved with three initials. B. A. R."

Cash took the bag. B.A.R.

"Will that help narrow down your suspect list?" Ross asked.

Cash nodded. When Boone Rasmussen had been arrested in Texas, his full name had been on the paperwork. Boone *Andrew* Rasmussen. B. A. R.

TY DREW Dusty under the grandstands, where it was dark and cool and somewhat quieter. People wandered past to the concessions or the restrooms, but with the rodeo in full swing, no one paid them any mind.

"All right," Dusty said the moment he let go of her. "What?"

"You should have told me that all this—" he waved a hand over her, taking in her new look "—was about *Boone Rasmussen.*"

She frowned. "Excuse me?"

"*Rasmussen?* Dusty, have you lost your mind?"

"Look Ty, I know you don't like Boone—"

"He's up to his neck in something. Have you forgotten that he almost killed you in the horse corral?"

"He said the gate latch was faulty."

"And you believe that?" Ty let out an exasperated sigh. "Slim, I think Boone had something to do with Clayton's murder and Waylon Dobbs's fire and his death."

"That's crazy," she snapped. "Why would Boone want to kill anyone?"

"It's all tied in somehow with Devil's Tornado," Ty said.

She stared at him. "You just don't want me going out with Boone. You're…" Her eyes widened. "You're… *jealous!*"

"*Jealous?*" He practically choked on the word. "This has nothing to do with how I feel about you."

"*Feel* about me?" she echoed.

She was close enough he could smell the light scent of her perfume. Slim, wearing perfume! Her lashes were dark with mascara, making the blue of her eyes seem bottomless.

This was Slim, he reminded himself. The girl next door whom he'd grown up with, looked out for, teased, tormented, adored. Slim. The pouty red lips, the palest blue eyes he'd ever seen, that adorable face. That body. He groaned. *His* Slim.

And all he wanted to do was throw her over his shoulder and haul her butt back to Antelope Flats. Either that or…kiss her.

He went with the kiss, drawing her to him. She was soft and lush-feeling in his arms. Her eyes lit with surprise in that instant before he dropped his mouth to hers.

He half expected her to pull away. Maybe even cuff him up side the head. That would be like the Dusty he knew and loved. Once he had her in his arms, once his mouth was on hers, he deepened the kiss.

Her reaction was nothing like he'd expected. No kick to the shin. No slugging him. She responded to his kiss. Not at first. But within a split second, her lips parted. Her body melted against his. All with stunning effect.

She let out a soft, almost pleased moan, then slowly, she drew back, eyes wide, her breath coming in short gasps.

He opened his mouth to speak. Nothing came out.

He was breathing hard, surprised and delighted and confused by what had just happened. He watched Dusty slowly run her tongue along her upper lip. She was still breathing hard, just like him, her face flushed with heat.

"Ty?" she whispered, staring at him as if she'd never seen him before.

He could only look at her, words lost on him.

"Why did you—" She broke off suddenly, her eyes narrowing. "Was *that*—" she waved an arm through the air "—about *Boone?*"

He scowled at her. "Hell, no. Listen to me, I know it sounds crazy, but I think Boone's drugging Devil's Tornado to make him perform better and I think Clayton and Waylon figured it out and that's why they're dead. Look, I know Cash didn't find any drugs when he tested Devil's Tornado, but don't you see the drug must be one that doesn't stay in the system long. He drugs the bull to work it up for the ride, then must give it something to bring it back down once the ride is over."

"*What?*" She looked shocked as she stepped back, her hand dropping to her shoulder bag.

Behind her, Boone came around the end of the grandstands. Had he been there the whole time listening, watching them?

Following Ty's surprised gaze, Dusty turned to look behind her. "Boone," she said, the name coming out on a surprised gasp.

"Dusty and I are having a private conversation," Ty said starting to step past Dusty to confront Boone, but Dusty grabbed his arm to stop him.

Rasmussen smiled at Dusty, completely ignoring him. "I have a surprise for you." He motioned for her to come with him.

Ty cursed. "Dusty—"

She gave him a warning look and slipped something into his hand. "I'll talk to you later, Ty," she said without looking back at him.

AT THE END of the first song, Flo Hubbard spotted Letty. Letty saw it happen—saw the instant of recognition, then the confusion.

Had her mother known she existed? Or had she been told, as some of the doctor's victims had been, that her baby was stillborn?

Flo turned to the bass guitarist and said something to him. He seemed a little surprised, but swung into another song. Flo looked at Letty, motioned for her to come around to the side of the stage. Leaning her guitar against one of the speakers, she disappeared from view.

Hal let go of Letty's hand.

"Come with me?" she pleaded.

His eyes met hers and locked for a long moment. He took her hand again, and they worked their way through the crowd to the side of the bandstand.

Flo shifted on her bare feet, her hands fluttering in

front of her as if she didn't know what to do with them. The band was playing something slow and melodious. Without discussing it, the three stepped away toward the concessionaires until the noise level was such that they would be able to hear each other.

Flo stopped, turning to look at Letty. "You're going to think I'm totally out of my mind…."

Letty shook her head. "I think you're my birth mother."

Flo seemed to slump, as if her bones had suddenly dissolved. She stumbled into a chair under the covered sitting area at a taco concession and sat down heavily, her gaze never leaving Letty's face. "It's not possible," she whispered.

Letty pulled up a chair next to her. Hal took one across from them. "It is possible." She glanced at Hal for help.

"Didn't you give birth twenty years ago on March 9 in Antelope Flats, Montana, at the clinic?"

Flo's green eyes filled with tears as she nodded. "Was that the name of the town? My van ran out of gas just outside of it. I was hitching into town when I went into labor. Just when I thought my luck had really run out, I was picked up by a doctor who worked at the clinic."

"That might not have been so lucky," Hal said.

Flo didn't seem to hear him. She appeared lost in the past as she said, "I was so young and scared, and it wasn't time yet for the baby to be born." She looked up at them. "But the baby was a boy, the doctor said. He was stillborn."

"Did you see your baby?" Hal asked.

She seemed to think for a moment, then shook her head. "The doctor put me out right before the baby was born. He told me something was wrong and wanted to spare me."

As Letty stared at her mother, Hal filled Flo in about the do-gooder doctor. "Let me guess. The doctor took care of everything, right?"

She nodded.

"I'm willing to bet, unless my eyes deceive me, that the doctor stole your baby and gave it to an older couple in town who couldn't have children," Hal continued. "Of course, DNA tests will be required to be absolutely sure…"

Flo let out a sudden laugh. "This is so freaky. I knew. I knew the moment I looked out into the crowd and saw you. I said, 'That's my kid.' I mean, how could I know something like that when I thought there was no way?"

"History has proven that a mother often knows her child on some level that we will never understand," Hal said quietly.

Flo nodded, studying her daughter's face. "You look exactly like I did at your age," she said with a laugh. "Sorry about that, kid."

Almost shyly, she reached out and placed her hand

over her daughter's. Letty intertwined her fingers with her mother's, and the two began to laugh and cry at the same time.

DUSTY FELT Boone slip his arm around her waist and pull her to him, his hand going to her shoulder bag.

Her head was spinning. Ty's kiss had left her weightless, trembling, excited and a little scared. She'd never felt anything like that. Still couldn't believe it. Ty?

She couldn't think. Everything was happening too fast. Ty thought Boone had been drugging Devil's Tornado? Was it possible the syringe she'd found and had just given to Ty had been used on the bull?

She didn't want to believe it of Boone, but she was reminded of his odd behavior at the Sheridan rodeo. She'd seen him jab the bull with something. A syringe? The one that she'd had in her purse all this time?

Boone suddenly stopped and turned her toward him. "You all right?" he asked, eyes narrowing.

"Fine." She forced a smile and added, "Great." Just great. For weeks, all she'd thought about was getting Boone to notice her. In her wildest dreams, he would ask her out and, if she got lucky, kiss her.

As he drew her toward him, she felt his hand part the top of her shoulder bag and his fingers dig inside. He was looking for the syringe! He must have seen her pick it up that night after the rodeo. All he'd ever wanted was the syringe!

He dropped his mouth to hers, his kiss hard and punishing as she felt him dig deeper in her bag.

TY FOUGHT TO BREATHE, the weight on his chest crushing his heart, his lungs, making him sick inside as he watched Boone kiss Dusty. She was right. He *was* jealous. Jealous as hell. But it was fear and anger that simmered inside him, making him want to do something stupid like bust this up right now. He could see that Boone had his hand in her purse as if looking for something.

Frowning, Ty looked down in his own hand and saw what Dusty had put there. A used syringe. He quickly stuck it into his jacket pocket, his hand shaking. That's what Boone was looking for. But what would Boone do when he didn't find it?

BOONE DREW BACK from the kiss, his dark eyes boring into hers for a long moment, before he shot Ty a look filled both with contempt and a warning as he drew Dusty toward the arena.

"You can watch the bull rides from the chutes with me," Boone said to Dusty, gripping her arm.

Ty saw Dusty wince and started to go after her but at that moment she glanced over her shoulder at him and mouthed, "Call Cash." Her look warned him. "Call Cash," she mouthed again. As she disappeared around the corner of the grandstands, Ty saw her shake off Boone's grip.

Boone looked angry but didn't reach for her again as she went with him willingly.

Oh, hell, what was she up to? Knowing her, she was going to try to get more proof. Where had she gotten the syringe? *When* had she gotten it? Had to have been that night at the Sheridan rodeo.

That look of shock on her face when Ty had told her his suspicions about Boone—it hadn't been because she didn't believe him, but because she *did!*

He took a breath, trying to think. Dusty was safe as long as she was at the rodeo around other people, right? He had the syringe in his pocket. If a lab could determine the drug inside, it might explain Devil's Tornado's behavior.

Unfortunately, it wouldn't be enough to put Boone Rasmussen behind bars. Not unless Boone drugged the bull again tonight and Ty could get a sample of the bull's blood right after the ride.

But if Boone had overheard Ty's conversation with Dusty, he wouldn't drug Devil's Tornado tonight. Unless it was already too late…

Over the loudspeaker, the final bull ride was being announced. Devil's Tornado in chute three. Ty didn't catch the bull rider's name as he hurried to the arena. Pulling his cell phone from his pocket, he dialed Sheriff Cash McCall's number.

HER LEGS STILL quivering, Dusty climbed up onto the fence, oblivious to the noise, the dust, the action in the arena in front of her.

"You're sure nothing's wrong?" Boone asked. His dark eyes drilled into her as if he could read her thoughts. She tried to smile, tried to act normal, whatever normal had been before today.

"I heard Coltrane warn you to stay clear of me. What is it he thinks he has against me?"

If he had heard Ty warn her about him, then Boone knew exactly what Ty thought he had against him. *"Nothing."*

Boone narrowed his dark eyes, a mocking smile curling his lips.

"It doesn't matter what Ty thinks," she said.

Boone didn't look convinced. "Stay here. "I'll be right back."

It wasn't her nature to stay. Especially when ordered. But she wanted Boone to believe that everything was all right. Ty would have called Cash. The police would come. This would be over soon. She just had to keep pretending that she liked Boone Rasmussen.

That was going to be the hard part.

She watched him rush over to the chute, saw his intense conversation with Lamar. Clearly, they were arguing. Boone looked furious. And…scared.

She stared at him, wandering what had ever attracted her to him. She touched a finger to her lips, remembering Ty's kiss. The feeling still burned inside. Ty. She smiled, still too surprised to believe it.

Now she knew what Ty had been doing that night

after the Sheridan rodeo. She looked across the arena, hoping to see him. By now, he would have called Cash. If her brother could get the local cops down here fast enough…

She didn't see Ty anywhere. Devil's Tornado was kicking up a ruckus inside the chute. Boone and Lamar were hanging over the chute now, the rider trying to get his rope wrapped around his hand.

All these weeks of dreaming about Boone and then Ty Coltrane kissed her and—

Her heart kicked up a beat just at the thought of Ty. She felt her face warm. She smiled and caught her lower lip in her teeth, feeling a little lightheaded. Ty Coltrane. Who would have known?

Suddenly, the chute banged open. Devil's Tornado lunged out, twisting and turning, a blur of movement. The rider tried to stay with him, but was quickly unseated. The pickup riders rode in an attempt to corner the bull. One of the horseback riders managed to get the bucking rope off, but it had little effect on Devil's Tornado.

Dusty stared at the bull as he stopped just feet from the fence where she sat. She could see now what Ty had seen. And Clayton and Waylon, had they seen it too?

Her pulse thundered in her ears. Had Boone killed to keep his secret? He didn't have that much to lose if he got caught drugging the bull, did he? He could just pack up and go somewhere else. Start over again. But murder…

The riders cornered Devil's Tornado, got a rope on him and dragged him out the exit chute.

She looked around for Boone, finally spotting him by Devil's Tornado. Past him, she saw Monte Edgewood climb into his pickup. He seemed to glance around as if looking for someone. His wife Sierra?

Dusty knew Monte Edgewood to say hello to on the street. He'd always seemed nice. She'd heard that he'd married a woman not much older than she was a while back. She'd only seen Sierra Edgewood a few times and felt sorry for her since Dusty knew only too well what it was like to have the whole county talking about you. He glanced at Boone, then slammed the door and drove off.

Because it was a three-day rodeo, the animals would be staying on the rodeo grounds. She could see the bucking horses in an adjacent pasture. The semitrucks and trailers were parked in a line along the back road.

Dusty saw Boone moving Devil's Tornado toward one of the corrals. She thought about when he'd kissed her and how she'd felt him digging in her purse. Looking for the syringe. Did he think she'd discarded it? Did he feel safe, even though he'd overheard Ty voicing his suspicions?

The lights went out, pitching the arena into darkness. In the distance, she thought she heard the wail of sirens but it was quickly lost in the boom of fireworks as the show got underway and some of the crowd began to wind their way out to their cars to beat the rush.

Dusty rubbed her arms, suddenly chilled at the

memory of the anger she'd seen in Boone's eyes. Was it possible this man she'd thought so intriguing was a murderer? She rubbed her arm where he'd grabbed it.

Fireworks burst in bright colors over her head. She looked toward the corral where Boone had been headed just moments ago. He and Devil's Tornado were gone!

Her gaze leaped to the semis parked out back. All three were there. He couldn't have gotten away. He must just have moved the bull to another corral. Or maybe the pasture out back.

She shivered in spite of herself as another volley of fireworks exploded, showering the night sky in blinding white.

Suddenly, she sensed someone behind her. The next instant, two strong hands grabbed her shoulders and hauled her off the fence and back into the shadows.

Chapter Thirteen

"You're coming with me and don't even try to argue," Ty whispered as he dragged Dusty off the fence and back into the dark shadows of the rodeo grounds as fireworks exploded all around them.

The moment he released her, Dusty swung around to face him. To his shock, she planted a quick kiss on his lips before he could speak again and hugged him fiercely.

Fireworks set the night sky ablaze. The boom reverberated in his chest.

"Why haven't you ever done that before?" she demanded drawing back to look at him.

"Done what?"

"Kissed me."

He quirked a smile at her. "What? And get my head knocked off? No way was I going to chance that."

As fireworks detonated overhead, she smiled at him in the brightly colored light. What he saw in her eyes bowled him over. He never dreamed that he and Slim—

"Who would have known?" they both said in unison, then laughed, instantly sobering at the distinct sound of sirens between bursts of fireworks.

"The police are on their way," he said and drew her closer. He had the syringe in his pocket. Once the police got blood from Devil's Tornado, they'd at least have a motive for Clayton and Waylon's murders.

The fireworks finale began, with one rocket blast of color and noise after another, ending in a thunderous boom.

Sparks drifted down, blinking out in the odd quiet that settled over the arena. Ty heard the distinct sound of a semitrailer door slam shut.

He and Dusty both turned in the direction of the trucks in time to see someone climb into the cab of the last one in line. Ty could make out the large shape of a bull in the back.

"Boone!" Dusty cried. "He's taking off with Devil's Tornado."

As the lights came on in the arena and people began to leave, the truck engine revved.

"We can't let Boone leave with that bull!" Dusty cried and took off running toward the semitruck before Ty could stop her.

He swore as she slipped through the chute fence, running ahead of him. He had to leap the fence, coming down hard in the soft earth.

Ty tried to keep his eye on the semi as Dusty closed the distance on it. On the other side of the truck, he saw boots as a second person moved along the back side of the trailer. The boots stopped at the driver's side door.

Dusty was almost to the semi, Ty right behind her. The motor suddenly revved even louder, but the truck didn't move as Dusty jumped up onto the running board and grabbed for the passenger side door handle.

Ty only got a glimpse of the boots on the other side of the truck before they disappeared as Dusty flung open the door and screamed.

LETTY HAD PARKED in the rodeo grounds parking lot as everyone else was leaving. Dusty had said she was meeting Boone near the concession stands after the rodeo was over, so Letty headed there. She was surprised to hear sirens. They sounded as if they were headed this way.

What kind of trouble had Dusty gotten herself into? Letty joked to herself. With an affectionate smile, she thought of her friend. She couldn't wait to tell Dusty the news. Not just about her birth mother, but about Hal, whom she was meeting later tonight.

The concessions were all boarded up and dark. With a wave of disappointment, Letty looked around but didn't see Dusty. Maybe she'd missed her. Letty chastised herself for not confiding in her friend sooner. But then, Letty hadn't known things would turn out so right.

Hugging herself, she glanced toward the back of the rodeo grounds and spotted a semitruck and trailer parked behind two others. She could hear the truck's motor running. Starting toward the line of semis, she heard the crunch of a boot sole on gravel and saw someone moving along the other side of the trucks.

"Boone?" she called softly. The figure behind the semitruck froze. Her heart kicked up a beat. She licked her lips and took a breath. "Boone?"

Behind her, two police cars came tearing into the parking lot. Several officers jumped out and ran toward a dark-colored pickup parked in the lot. Boone's truck?

At a sound behind her, Letty swung back around. The figure behind the semitruck was gone!

Run! She barely got the thought out before he came out of the dark, his arm locking around her neck so quickly she didn't have time to react. She opened her mouth to scream but his free hand clamped over it.

She struggled, kicking and clawing as he dragged her deeper into the darkness.

"Keep fighting and I'll have to hurt you," a male voice whispered hoarsely in her ear, his breath hot, his arm tightened on her neck, cutting off her air.

She stopped struggling.

DUSTY'S SCREAM was lost in the sound of the sirens.

"Wait!" Ty yelled after her. But that, too, was lost in her scream.

Ty was right behind her, leaping up to grab the edge of the door, afraid the truck would take off and kill them both.

Dusty shoved back against him, her mouth a perfect *O,* her eyes filled with horror in the dash lights of the truck cab.

Ty caught her and held her with one arm as he ducked down to look inside. Lamar's huge shape was behind the wheel, his head lolling back against the seat as if resting, his eyes wide with terror, his throat cut from ear to ear, his shirt crimson with his blood.

"Son of a bitch," Ty said and pulled Dusty from the running board to the ground. She was shaking hard. He wrapped his arms around her, burying his face into the hollow of her neck, his mind racing. He'd seen the killer's boots moving along the back side of the truck.

"I saw Boone arguing with Lamar before Devil's Tornado's ride," Dusty said glancing back at the semi. Boone. Where the hell was he?

"We have to find the cops," Ty said, turning to look back toward the arena. The grandstands were empty now, smoke from the fireworks show hanging heavy in the air.

"Boone is long gone," Ty said trying to still Dusty's trembling.

She shook her head and stepped from his arms to move along the side of the steel semitrailer. "He wouldn't leave without Devil's Tornado."

Through the narrow slit openings, Ty could see a bull standing inside the trailer.

But Boone and Devil's Tornado were gone.

DUSTY COULDN'T quit shaking. She stared at the bull in the stock trailer. Boone had fooled them! He'd put a different bull in the trailer. He'd made them think he was the one in the semitruck trying to get away with Devil's Tornado, get away with what he'd done. Instead, he'd disappeared with the bull—after he killed Lamar.

She shuddered at the memory of Lamar, his throat cut.

Ty put an arm around her. "Come on, Slim. Let's find the cops."

She snuggled into him. Ty had always been there for her. What about that had she equated with a lack of mystery, no surprises? She'd known him since she was a child, and yet she didn't know him. Not the man who'd kissed her. Not the man who made her quake in his arms. Nor the strong, capable man who held her now.

"How did Boone get the bull out of here without us seeing him?" Dusty asked, turning to stare at the line of semis.

Ty shook his head. She could tell he was wondering the same thing she was. Boone might be a lot of things, but he was no magician. So didn't that mean that he and the bull had to still be here somewhere?

Or maybe he'd left with the crowd, disappearing among the other cowboy hats. And Devil's Tornado? Where was the bull?

She shivered, chilled to the bone at the thought of

what Boone was capable of. Instinctively, she'd known he was dangerous. That had been the attraction. The unknown. Letty had tried to warn her, but Dusty hadn't listened.

They hadn't gone more than a few yards from the trucks when Dusty sensed someone behind them. She saw Ty tense and spin around, pushing her to one side to protect her with his body.

Before Ty could get an arm up, Boone raised a gun and brought the butt end down on the side of Ty's head.

"No!" she cried as Ty crumpled to her feet and Boone Rasmussen grabbed her arm and jerked her to him.

"Where is the syringe?" Boone demanded, grabbing her shoulder bag and dumping it on the ground while keeping a firm grip on Dusty's arm.

"Ty," Dusty cried. He didn't answer, didn't move. She could hear the sirens again, only this time they seemed to be going away from the rodeo grounds.

Boone kicked away the larger objects that had fallen from the bag, then jerked Dusty to him hard. "*Where* is the syringe?"

"I threw it away," she said.

"You're a worse liar than your boyfriend."

He dragged her over to Ty and pulled her down next to him as he quickly went through Ty's pockets.

Questions ran through her mind: why would Boone stay around here after killing Lamar to get the syringe? Was he crazy?

But Dusty quickly forgot Boone as she touched Ty's face. He felt ice-cold. "You bastard, you killed him!"

Boone let out an oath as he found the syringe in Ty's pocket. Clutching it in one hand, he dragged her up with the other. As he tried to stuff the syringe into his own pocket, Dusty launched herself at him. The last thing she remembered was seeing his fist, feeling it connect with her temple just before the earth came up to meet her.

BOONE KNEW he shouldn't have been surprised that things were going so badly. Hell, hadn't he blown every chance he'd ever gotten? Why should this time be any different?

He stared down at Ty Coltrane. Dusty lay beside him, out like a light.

What the hell should he do now? He looked to the road past the rodeo grounds and blinked as he saw his pickup go racing by. Two cop cars were in hot pursuit. What the hell? *Someone had stolen his pickup?*

He felt in his pocket. How was that possible? He had his keys. Who in his right mind would go to the trouble to hot-wire and steal an old pickup?

The sound of the sirens grew fainter and fainter, the flashing lights disappearing in the distance.

How was he supposed to get out of here now?

The arena lights were still on. From this corner of darkness, he couldn't see anyone left around the rodeo grounds. Monte had left earlier. Apparently none of the cops had stayed behind—both police cars were chasing a car thief instead. Lucky for him, except now he had no vehicle to get the hell out of here.

What had the cops been doing here in the first place? All he could assume was that Coltrane had called them, planning to hand over the syringe—and Boone. That would explain why they were hot after his pickup.

Coltrane moaned. He wasn't dead. Boone was surprised at his relief. He couldn't stand the sight of Coltrane. What did he care if he was dead? But his body would be a complication Boone didn't need right now. He had enough complications.

He touched the syringe in his pocket. He had taken Devil's Tornado out to a field a quarter mile from the rodeo grounds. The bull wouldn't be found for a while and by then, there would be nothing *to* find. Hell, what did the cops have on him, anyway?

Nothing. He had the syringe. There was no evidence he'd been drugging the bull. Coltrane might have him jailed for assault, but other than that the cops couldn't prove anything.

Dusty was starting to come around. He knew she would start screaming her head off the moment she did. He didn't want to be around when that happened, he thought, glancing back at the semitruck and trailer.

He wished there was another way as he moved to the hulking shadow of the semi and swung open the driver's side door.

At first, his mind refused to accept what he was

seeing. Blood. Lamar. So much blood. His stomach did a slow sickening roll. He stumbled back, fighting to keep from throwing up. His head was reeling. Someone had killed Lamar? Who—

He never saw the tire iron. Or the hand that wielded it. A blinding pain ripped through this skull an instant before the darkness as Boone pitched forward.

DUSTY OPENED HER EYES and was instantly assaulted by the smell, the noise and the jarring movement. She blinked, her head aching. Her hands and ankles were bound with duct tape. Another strip had been put across her mouth, forcing her to breathe through her nose.

The darkness stank of manure and hay, and she couldn't be sure which she was lying in.

Only a little light bled in through the slits along the side of the semitrailer as it rattled down the highway through the dark. At the front of the trailer where she lay was blackness. No headlights from other vehicles on the highway illuminated the interior.

She tried to sit up, but fell over as the semi took a curve. Pushing with her feet, she managed to work her way into the corner and get her back against the walls of the trailer, her eyes finally adjusting to the dizzying darkness.

At the far end of the trailer by the door, she saw a shape. She stared until her eyes burned. The dark shape moved and Dusty let out a muffled cry as she realized it was a bull. Devil's Tornado?

Fear paralyzed her. She could feel the bull looking at her. She'd seen what Devil's Tornado had tried to do to the cowboys in the arena after the bucking rigging had been removed. The bull was a killer. He'd stomp her to death or gore her or—

Devil's Tornado seemed to sway before her eyes, then dropped to his knees, going all the way to the floor of the trailer as he lay down as docile as an old cow.

Closer, Dusty heard another sound. Movement and a low moan. She looked to her left, to the adjacent dark corner of the trailer. Ty?

Her eyes widened in horror!

Letty—her hands bound, her mouth taped, her eyes wide and terrified stared back at her from the darkness!

What was Letty doing here? And where was Ty? She searched the darkness, but quickly realized that she and Letty were alone with a bull in the back of the semi-trailer headed for God only knew where with a killer at the wheel. Where was Boone taking them?

Frantically, Dusty began to work at the tape on her mouth, pushing it with her tongue as she rubbed at the corner with her shoulder along the rough edge of her jacket. She could feel the edge start to peel back. Her skin chafed from the effort, but she had to be able to talk to Letty. To reassure her. To reassure herself that somehow they were going to get out of this.

BLINDED BY the bright light, Ty Coltrane closed his eyes and tried to sit up. "Where's Dusty?"

"Easy," one of the policemen standing over him warned. "You've got quite the knot on your head. We've called for an ambulance. Can you tell us who hit you?"

"Boone Rasmussen. I have to find Dusty," Ty said, pushing to his feet. His gaze went to the spot where the semitrucks and trailers had been. One was missing. "He's got her. He's taken the truck." Ty turned to head for his pickup, but one of the cops grabbed his arm.

"Hold on," the officer said. "You're not going anywhere. We need to ask you some questions."

Ty jerked free and probably would have ended up in jail if he hadn't stopped to watch a helicopter set down in the middle of the arena—and see Sheriff Cash McCall climb out of it.

"Cash!" he called as the sheriff ran toward him. "Rasmussen has Dusty. I think he took her in one of the Edgewood semitrucks. Lamar is dead."

Cash began barking orders, starting with getting an APB out on the semitruck, then turned to the police officers in confusion. "Did you just get here? I called you hours ago."

One of the officers, Sgt. Mike Johnson, stepped forward. "After your call, we came to the rodeo grounds, spotted Boone Rasmussen's pickup, based on the description and plate number you gave us, and pursued the pickup as the driver gave chase."

Ty stared at the cop. "But Rasmussen was here with me and Dusty."

The cop nodded. "We finally forced the driver of the pickup off the road about twelve miles out of town and took her into custody. It wasn't Boone Rasmussen, but a woman by the name of Sierra Edgewood."

"Sierra was driving Rasmussen's pickup?" Ty asked in surprise.

"She'd been drinking," the cop said. "Told us that she thought her husband, Monte Edgewood, had set us on her and that she had kept going out of fear of what her husband would do to her if she was caught and turned over to him." The cop looked to Cash. "Is there any basis for her concerns about her husband?"

"Not that I know of," Cash said. "She had a key to Rasmussen's pickup?"

The cop nodded. "A single key. She said she'd had it made one day when she'd borrowed the pickup. Planned to use it to get away from her abusive husband."

"No way," Ty spoke up. "She was a diversion so Boone could get away." His head ached. He rubbed a hand over his face. "But why would Sierra Edgewood help Boone Rasmussen?"

"Good question," Cash said.

From over by the other two semis, one of the police officers yelled, "I've got a body over here."

"His name is Lamar Nichols," Cash said after taking a look. "If you have any more questions for Mr. Coltrane, they will have to wait. It appears the killer might have my sister. Don't try to apprehend him if you find him. Wait for me." He looked to Ty. "Let's find Dusty."

The two ran to the highway patrol helicopter and buckled up as the chopper took off.

"Boone could be headed in any direction," Cash said. "He's originally from Texas. I'd think he would head south on 191 along the Gallatin River."

Ty tried to calm the panic rising in him as Cash told the pilot to head south toward West Yellowstone and the Idaho border. Had Boone taken Dusty? What would he do to her? Was she even still alive?

Ty stared down at the dark ribbon of highway and river below them. Who knew where Rasmussen would go. Or what he would do. Ty tried to concentrate and not panic.

Would he go back to Texas? Or hide somewhere? "He'll have to get rid of the semi for something less conspicuous," Ty said out loud. But why take Dusty? "She has to be a hostage in case he's cornered and has to bargain his way out."

"We can only hope that's the case," Cash said. "That means he will want to keep her alive."

Cash checked in with the highway patrol and sheriff's departments on the ground. Ty could tell from this side of the conversation that there was still no sign of the semi.

Ty thought about what Cash had told the Bozeman police. It was believed that Rasmussen had killed three people to keep his secret—Clayton T. Brooks, Waylon Dobbs and Lamar Nichols. He was desperate. He could do anything.

Cash took another call on the radio. Ty saw him frown and held his breath, terrified it was news of Dusty. Bad news.

"Is it…?" he asked.

Cash shook his head. "No word on Rasmussen or Dusty."

Cash got another call and took it as Ty watched the highway below them for the semi.

Cash clicked off and Ty could tell from his expression that this call hadn't been good news. "It was one of the roughstock producers in Texas I'd contacted about Rasmussen." Cash frowned. "Did you know that Lamar was Rasmussen's half brother?"

Ty shook his head.

"If Rasmussen had one allegiance, it would be to his own blood, wouldn't you think? And given that he'd brought Lamar up here with him from Texas, given him a job…"

"Unless he killed him to keep him from talking," Ty said.

Cash shook his head as if struggling with the same thing Ty was. If Rasmussen hadn't killed Lamar, then who did that leave?

Cash let out an oath. "You aren't thinking what I'm thinking?"

"That Sierra was a diversion, but not for Boone Rasmussen?" Ty said.

Cash swore again and leaned toward the pilot. "Take us to Antelope Flats as fast as you can get this thing to go."

Chapter Fourteen

Dusty managed to peel back the edge of the tape on her mouth. She used her tongue to free all but one corner.

"Letty!" she cried as she scooted toward the opposite corner to her friend. Tears shone in Letty's eyes. "Turn around and I'll try to free your hands."

Dusty squirmed around until she had her back to Letty's. She began to work at the tape around Letty's wrists. It was slow going. As she worked, she told Letty everything, about Ty and the kiss, about Boone, about the syringe she'd picked up in the corral that night in Sheridan and had forgotten about. She left out the part about Lamar, not wanting to scare Letty even worse.

She almost had Letty's hands free when the truck slowed, throwing them both off balance. The semi turned onto a bumpy dirt road. Dusty worked her way close to Letty again and tugged faster at the duct tape holding Letty's wrists together.

Dusty could feel time slipping away. The semi

moved slowly along the dirt road, giving her the feeling that it wasn't going far. She had to get Letty free and quickly.

As the truck began to slow down even more, the last of the tape pulled free.

Letty reached up and jerked the tape from her mouth with a cry of pain then hurriedly began tugging at the tape on Dusty's wrists. She talked ninety miles an hour, telling Dusty about having been stolen from her birth mother, about meeting Hal Branson, finding her birth mother and coming to the rodeo to tell her best friend.

As Letty freed Dusty's wrists, the two hugged fiercely, both crying in relief and fear, before quickly working to free their ankles.

As the truck rolled to a stop, Devil's Tornado stirred at the rear of the trailer.

A yard light came on. Light cut through the slits in the side of the trailer.

Dusty blinked, seeing something she hadn't been able to earlier. There was something lying on the other side of Devil's Tornado. Ty?

She scrambled to her feet and rushed toward the bull, forgetting about her safety in her fear that she would find Ty lying dead at the back of the semitrailer.

But Devil's Tornado didn't move. Just watched her with a disinterested, almost too calm look. *He's drugged,* Dusty thought, an instant before she saw the cowboy stretched out on the floor next to the bull.

It wasn't Ty, she saw at once. Behind Dusty, Letty

let out a small cry. "Boone? If Boone's in here with us, then who—"

Letty didn't get to finish as the door of the trailer clanged open and the two stood staring down at Monte Edgewood—and the gun he held in his hand, the barrel pointed in their direction.

"WELL, AREN'T YOU two clever getting loose," Monte said congenially. "Come on down from there."

"I don't understand what's going on," Dusty said as she looked from Monte's big open face to the gun in his hand. Everyone in the county liked Monte Edgewood. Some had wondered if he'd lost his mind when he married a woman half his age. No one had ever really liked Sierra. But if anything, they were kinder to Monte because of their dislike for his young wife.

"Come on down, girls," Monte said and motioned with the gun for Dusty to step down first. Letty followed, hanging on to the back of Dusty's jacket.

He herded them toward a small old barn. Dusty could see the moon peeking in and out of the clouds overhead and tried to estimate how long they'd been in the back of the semitrailer. She didn't recognize the barn. It was old and crumbling and could have been located anywhere in Montana, or for that matter, in Idaho or Wyoming.

But she got the feeling that it was on Monte's property as he swung open the door and ushered them both inside. Straw bales were stacked along one wall. An old lantern sat on a bench nearby, the flickering flame lighting the small interior.

Dusty stumbled in with Letty at her side as Monte forced them back against the straw bales. There was little else in the barn. She tried to see past the lantern light to dark corners, looking for something she could use as a weapon. There was no doubt in her mind that Monte Edgewood intended to kill them.

"Where is Ty?" she asked, afraid of the answer. But she had to know.

"At the rodeo, where we left him." Monte patted her shoulder. "Don't worry. He's fine. By now, the police have found him. He'll live."

Dusty felt Letty shudder next to her, the words, *he'll live* hanging in the air as if to say Ty would live, unlike her and Letty.

"Mr. Edgewood—" Letty began.

"Call me Monte," he said. "You're the Arnolds' girl, right?"

Letty didn't answer. "What are you going to do with us?"

"Not me. Boone." He made a disappointed face. "He was like a son to me. I trusted him. I took him into my home. I taught him about the roughstock business. I would have given him anything." Monte let out a laugh that chilled Dusty to the bone. "Hell, I *did* give him everything." His eyes narrowed, darkened; the hand holding the gun seemed to quiver. "Including my wife."

Dusty took Letty's hand and squeezed it, trying to reassure her when Dusty herself was scared speechless.

Monte looked up at them as if he'd been gone for a moment. He blinked, seemed to refocus. "Boone was such a fool. If he'd just come to me with his plan. Hell, I would have helped him. But he didn't trust me." He shook his head. "Trust. It all comes down to trust, doesn't it?"

Dusty thought about making a run for it with Letty, but she knew Monte would chase them down even if they split up, which Dusty wasn't about to do.

She listened, thought she heard something, a faint hum in the distance. A vehicle? Ty had called her brother. Cash would be looking for her. Only both Ty and Cash would think that Boone had her—not Monte Edgewood.

"It's funny," Monte said more to himself than Dusty and Letty. "You never know what you will do. You think you know yourself. You have this image of the kind of person you are. Then something happens. You have everything you've ever wanted and more, and someone comes along and offers you a chance to be famous. And even though you know it's a false kind of rise to fame, you latch on to the dream because you want so desperately to be a part of it."

Dusty let her gaze scan the barn for a weapon. She had no idea what Monte was talking about. He sounded half-crazy. That scared her as much as the gun. The hum in the air she'd heard earlier seemed to be getting louder. Not a vehicle. More like a plane. Or a helicopter!

She spotted a pitchfork by the door and an old ax handle on the floor in the corner, nothing else. Neither was close enough to get to them before Monte fired the gun.

But the lantern was only a few yards away on the other side of Letty.

Dusty realized that Monte had stopped talking. "What was the dream?" she asked hurriedly, latching on to the only word she could recall.

He frowned. "A bull that would make everyone in the country remember the name Edgewood Roughstock Company. Devil's Tornado."

Everyone will remember that name now, Dusty thought.

Monte had stopped talking again and was listening now, his expression making it clear that he, too, heard the sound of what could have been a helicopter outside, coming closer.

"I'm sorry it has to end like this," he said. "Boone was a bad seed. It was my fault for letting him infect me and my wife. Once he is gone… I'm just sorry that he killed so many people before he was stopped." Monte raised the gun, pointing it at Letty.

Dusty still had hold of her friend's hand. "No!" Dusty cried, stepping in front of Letty to lunge for the lantern Monte had left on a small bench nearby. She flung the lantern in Monte's direction as she dragged Letty to the barn floor with her.

The deafening sound of a gunshot boomed in the empty barn, sending a flock of pigeons flapping down from the rafters overhead. Dust filled the air an instant after the lantern ricocheted off Monte's arm. Glass exploded as the lantern hit the floor. Fuel and flames skittered up the dry wood wall, setting the straw bales on fire.

Dusty and Letty scrambled to their feet. But Monte was blocking the door, the gun raised as he tried to take aim at them. They dove for the back of the barn, realizing too late there was no way out as flames lapped at the dried wood of the old barn, thick smoke quickly filling the small space.

Dusty's eyes burned as she pulled the corner of her jacket up to cover her mouth and nose. Letty did the same. They were trapped. There was no place to run. No place to hide. Monte raised the gun.

Something moved behind Monte. Dusty felt her heart jump, praying it would be help. Boone Rasmussen materialized in the doorway.

"Monte!" He picked up the pitchfork and called again. "Monte!"

Monte turned slowly, seeming surprised to see Boone, even more surprised to see the pitchfork in his hand. The older man shook his head, as if he knew Boone wouldn't use it. He raised the gun and fired.

Boone stumbled back a step and looked down at the blood pouring out of the bullet hole in his chest. Then he raised the pitchfork and lunged at Monte.

Monte fired again. Through the smoke, Dusty saw Boone fall to his knees. Behind him, Ty appeared like a mirage from out of the darkness in the barn doorway.

The fire crackled all around them, sweeping up the walls, setting the roof on fire.

Dusty called to Ty to watch out as Monte raised the gun to fire at him. She rushed Monte, Letty beside her. They hit him hard from behind. He stumbled and went down.

Ty grabbed Dusty and Letty and dragged them out of the inferno. Dusty caught sight of her brother as Cash pulled Boone's body out as charred timbers began to fall from overhead.

Cash started to go back for Monte, But it was too late. The roof collapsed in a shower of sparks and smoke. Dusty buried her face in Ty's chest as flames engulfed what was left of the barn—and Monte Edgewood.

Chapter Fifteen

Dusty felt as if she were in a fog as they left the Edgewood ranch and headed for the clinic in town.

Boone had already been pronounced dead at the
scene. Parts of the barn still burning. The fire department and coroner had been called.

Cash had the helicopter take Dusty and Letty to
the clinic, sending Ty along with them. Although
everyone involved in the case seemed to be dead or,
in Sierra's case, in jail, Cash wasn't taking any
chances.

Cash stopped by the hospital with questions for
Dusty and Ty. Dusty told her brother about the night
after the rodeo when someone had followed her home.

"It was Boone," Dusty said. "I didn't know it at the
time, but he must have seen me pick up the syringe. I
stuck it in my purse and forgot all about it."

"I've seen all the stuff you have in that purse, so I
can believe that," Cash said. "But why pick it up at all?"

Dusty shot him a duh look. "One of the horses could

have stepped on it. Any rancher would pick it up and pocket it."

"Probably why I became a sheriff," he said.

"Sierra is singing like a canary from her jail cell in Bozeman," Cash said. "She said she'd awakened the night Clayton T. Brooks was murdered to see her husband coming in from the far pasture, his shirt and jeans covered in blood. She'd pretended to be asleep as he put the clothes into the washer and showered before returning to bed."

"So she knew," Ty said shaking his head.

"When she'd heard Clayton had been murdered and that Cash thought Clayton had come out to the Edgewood Roughstock Ranch the night he died, Sierra still couldn't believe Monte had killed him," Cash said. "At least that's her story. She said she thought Monte was covering for Boone."

"What about Waylon's murder?" Ty asked.

"Sierra says Waylon had been by the ranch the day he died," Cash said. "She'd seen Waylon and Monte out in the yard arguing."

"So you think Waylon tried to blackmail Monte?"

"Appears that way," Cash said. "According to Sierra, Monte had come into the house upset. Later he left and when he came back, she smelled smoke on him. But she also smelled smoke on Boone later that night when she went to his bed. Boone said it was from Lamar smoking in his truck. We still don't know how Boone's watch ended up in the ashes at Waylon's house if Monte set the fire."

Dusty frowned. "I might. You know that night at the rodeo in Sheridan, the night Boone chased me home? I saw Boone drop something on the ground. At the time I just saw something glitter. It must have been his watch because Monte picked it up and pocketed it."

"Then used the watch to try to frame Boone for Waylon's murder and the fire," Cash said.

"So Sierra really did take Boone's truck to get away from Monte?" Ty asked.

Cash nodded. "She says she realized he knew about her and Boone and that she feared he planned to kill her, too."

"Why?" Letty asked. "Why would someone like Monte Edgewood do this?"

"Greed, pride, the need to be somebody," Cash said. "He saw that Devil's Tornado could make him famous. Once he found out that Boone was drugging the bull, he chose to kill to cover the deception."

"By killing?" Ty asked. "He couldn't possibly think he could get away with it."

"Once he found out about Sierra and Boone, he planned to frame Boone for all the murders," Dusty said, remembering what Monte had said in the barn last night.

"According to Sierra, under the contract Monte had with Boone, if something happened to Boone, Monte would get Devil's Tornado," Cash said. "Except it turns out that Devil's Tornado is really a docile bull named Little Joe."

"What happens to the Edgewood Roughstock Ranch and Little Joe?" Dusty asked.

"Sierra inherits it all," Cash said. "She already has a lawyer looking into selling everything, lock, stock and barrel. I would imagine that will be the last we see of her."

"So it's over," Ty said.

"Seems that way," Cash agreed.

Dr. Taylor Ivers came back into the room to give Letty and Dusty some salve for the slight blistering they'd suffered on their faces. She'd already treated them for smoke inhalation and said they could go.

Dusty thanked the doctor. Taylor was part of the Mc-Call family in an extended way. Everyone had thought Taylor would leave town after everything that had happened, but she seemed determined to stay on at the clinic.

Taylor seemed to be lightening up a little. Dusty had heard that Taylor and her sister Anna Austin VanHorn McCall even had lunch once a week now.

"You need a ride home?" Cash asked Dusty.

"I borrowed a pickup from a friend," Ty said quickly. "I'll take her and Letty home."

Cash smiled and nodded, giving his sister a hug before he left.

When Ty pulled up in front of Letty's motel, Hal Branson was waiting for her.

Hal had been out of his mind when she hadn't shown up for their date and, after talking to the police, had driven clear to Antelope Flats in the middle of the night because he'd been so worried about her. The last time he'd talked to Letty, she was headed for the rodeo to meet Dusty—and Hal had feared she'd met up with more than Dusty.

Dusty couldn't have handpicked a man more perfect for Letty, she thought, when she met Hal. She could just imagine their children. And seeing the joy in both of their faces, Dusty had a feeling marriage and children wouldn't be that far off.

Hal offered to make coffee since the sun would be coming up soon. He and Letty went into the house behind the motel office.

"I'll give you a ride home," Ty offered. "Unless you want to stay here and have coffee."

Dusty shook her head. "Three's a crowd." She reached over and took one of the keys off the board behind the motel desk. "Looks like No. 9 is empty," she said and tossed the key to him.

TY STARED DOWN at the key, then up at Slim. He'd never been so thrown off balance by any woman in his life. His gaze met hers.

"Well?" she asked.

"Slim—"

"I know. It's been one hell of a night. I have no intention of going home and having to tell this story again." Her eyes locked with his. "Nor do I plan to spend what's left of this night alone in my bed." She smiled. "I already told Cash I wouldn't be coming home tonight. You going to try to make a liar out of me?"

"You sure about this, Slim?"

"More sure than I have ever been about anything in my life," she said leaning into him to kiss him. "And you know me."

He chuckled. "Oh, yeah, I know you, Slim." And he was about to get to know her better. "But I have to tell you that I always pictured us married first, me carrying you over the threshold of our new house."

"Really?" She smiled. "How long would it take to build this house?"

"Six months, at least."

"Great," she said, taking the motel room key from his hand. "That will give us plenty of time to get to know each other better. Starting tonight."

She started to walk past him, but he reached out and pulled her to him, kissing her as he took the motel room key.

"It's not the same as our own home, mind you," he said as he swung her up in his arms and shoved open the door. "But for tonight, it will have to do."

DUSTY WAS TREMBLING when he set her down in motel room No. 9. Nine for luck, she thought as she looked up at him. A chill rippled across her skin, an ache in her belly. This was Ty, a boy she'd known all her life.

Only as she looked at him, she realized he wasn't a boy anymore. She was staring into the eyes of a man. A man whom she suspected would continue to surprise her until the day she died.

A shudder quaked through her as he took her in his arms and kissed her, deepening the kiss as he molded his body to hers.

"Ty," she moaned against his wonderful mouth.

His large hands took her shoulders and backed her up until she was pressed against the wall. His mouth dropped to hers again. The sensation was like fireworks exploding through her body.

He rested his hand on the curve of her hip. Snaked his fingers up her rib cage and slipped it under the edge of her bra. A soft sigh escaped her lips as his warm hand cupped her breast. He bent to press his mouth against her throat, sending a shiver of kisses along the rim of her ear. His tongue licked across her warm skin as his hands skimmed over her body, as if he were memorizing every inch, tasting every inch.

Her fingers dug into his muscled back as he carried her over to the bed. "Slim," he whispered, then drew back. "Would you rather I call you Dusty?" he asked, so serious it made her laugh.

She shook her head. She was his Slim and they both knew it.

She didn't remember him taking off her clothes. Or

her taking off his. But suddenly they were naked, their bodies melding together as they rolled around on the bed, laughing and kissing, his blue eyes a flame burning over her bare skin, hotter than the fire in the barn.

His mouth dropped to her breast and she thought she would die from the sheer pleasure of it. She buried her hands in his thick hair, moaning as he gently bit down on her hard nipple, arching against him, loving the feel of flesh to flesh. Loving Ty.

He made love to her slowly, gently, with a kind of awe, as if amazed that she had given herself to him so completely. She found even the pain of her first time was pleasurable. They made love again as the sun rose on another day, all the horror of what they'd been through slipping away like clouds after a rainstorm.

In Ty's arms, she found everything she'd dreamed of and more. He fulfilled her every fantasy as if he knew exactly what she wanted. What she needed. Later, she propped herself up on one elbow and looked down at him, surprised that she felt no embarrassment.

"Your father is going to think we're too young to get married," Ty said, running his thumb along her lower lip.

She kissed the rough pad of his thumb and shook her head. "My father will be delighted."

Ty didn't look so sure about that.

"You'll see. I know my father." She fell silent for a moment, thinking about Asa. "Can I tell you something?"

"You can tell me anything, Slim."

"I think he's dying."

Ty sat up in surprise. "Oh, honey."

She nodded and brushed at the tears that blurred her eyes. "I saw something in his expression at the last family dinner. I think he planned to tell us all, but then Cash had to leave." She bit down on her lower lip as Ty pulled her to him, holding her tightly in his arms.

They made love again, slow and sweet. She fell into a deep sleep in Ty's arms, only to be awakened by the phone late the next day.

Ty answered it, listened, then handed it to her, his face set in a grim line that frightened her.

"Dusty?" It was Shelby. What was her mother doing calling her? The only way she would have known where to find her was from Cash—and there was no way he would have told Shelby about what had happened last night.

"What's wrong?" Dusty asked, sitting up, thinking it might be about her father.

"You have to come home," Shelby said.

Dusty was ready to launch into a speech about how she was twenty-one and she didn't have to explain herself when Shelby said, "I wouldn't have called you, Dusty, but it's your father."

Dusty gripped the phone tighter.

"He wants everyone to come out to the ranch," Shelby said. "Rourke, Brandon and J.T. are already here with their wives. Cash and Molly are on their way. You're welcome to bring Ty with you. This concerns everyone who your father—" her voice broke "—loves."

Dusty could hear her mother crying softly.

"We'll be right there."

ONCE EVERYONE WAS SEATED around the large dining room table, Asa McCall stood. It took all the strength he had, but he wanted to do this standing. He didn't want them to see how weak he was. Soon enough, they would know.

"I appreciate you all coming on such short notice," he said, looking around the table at each of them, his sons and their wives or soon-to-be-wives, Dusty and Ty. He'd always hoped his headstrong daughter would realize that the man of her dreams lived just up the road.

There was so much he wanted to say to them.

To think he'd almost lost Dusty last night. Cash had filled him in, no doubt leaving out many of the more frightening details. The thought that Dusty might not be here with them practically dropped him to his knees.

Shelby reached over and took his hand, squeezed it and smiled reassuringly at him. The love of his life. Strong, just like her daughter. He thanked God for that.

He cleared his throat and began the story about his friend Charley and the land deal, telling the story quickly, simply.

He knew his children would understand the consequences at once. They were too smart not to.

When he'd finished, J.T. had his head in his hands. Everyone looked stricken.

"I don't see how you could have let something like this happen," J.T. said, then shook his head.

"It happened," Rourke cut in. "The question is, what can we do?"

Asa shook his head and suddenly had to sit down. "We haven't enough money or capital to buy him out. The mineral rights are worth more than the land."

"There must be some way to stop this," Cash said. "Have you talked to a lawyer?"

"The contract cannot be broken," Asa said. "I've already tried to buy back the mineral rights. He wouldn't sell to me even if I could raise that much money."

"But we're at the north end of the coal fields," Rourke said. "There might not even be any coalbed methane gas at this end of the valley. That mineral rights contract might not be worth the paper it's written on."

"It seems Charley's son is willing to take that chance," Asa said.

"It will change the ranch, but we will still own the land," Dusty spoke up, as if waiting for worse news. He'd seen the look in her eyes when she'd come into the room. She knew he was dying. Like her mother, she probably could also see how weak he was and that this was taking every ounce of his strength.

He smiled down the table at her, grateful to have such a daughter.

"There will be roads all over to the gas well heads," Rourke was saying. "Even if they don't find gas, they will drill for months. Maybe even years, putting in roads, ruining the land."

"Yesterday, I received a letter in the mail that Charley's son has sold the mineral rights lease," Asa said and looked down the table at his youngest son. "It was bought up by Mason VanHorn."

He watched Brandon look over at his wife, Anna VanHorn McCall, in surprise. Asa had been trying to come to terms with the fact that Brandon had gone against his wishes and married Anna. He'd feared that the long-standing feud between the McCalls and the VanHorns would end up destroying his son's life. When he'd seen the letter and found out that Mason VanHorn had bought up the mineral rights lease for McCall land, Asa knew his worst fear had come true.

Only Mason VanHorn had the kind of money to buy up the lease. Asa was thankful he wouldn't live long enough to see a VanHorn drilling on McCall land.

"Is that true?" Brandon asked Anna.

She rose slowly from her seat at the table. She was a beautiful woman, just as her mother had been. Reaching into her pocket, she pulled out a thick envelope of papers and handed them to her husband. "These are for Asa."

Brandon took them and, without looking at them, passed them down the table to Asa.

"It's true, my father purchased the mineral rights

lease," Anna said. "It was his wedding present to me and Brandon." She met Asa's gaze. "And a peace offering, so that the children and grandchildren of the McCalls and the VanHorns can finally live in peace."

Asa felt his hands begin to shake as he read the papers, his eyes filling with tears of gratitude as he looked down the table at his daughter-in-law. He could only shake his head in disbelief, his sworn enemy coming to his rescue.

The irony wasn't lost on him. VanHorn had made a fortune in gas wells—something Asa had sworn would never be found on his ranch. And in the end? VanHorn had used that fortune to buy back Asa's soul from the devil. In return, Mason VanHorn asked for nothing. Nothing, after all the years of the bad blood between them.

"Thank you," Asa said. "I look forward to the day when I can thank your father in person."

"But there's more, isn't there?" Cash said. "More you need to tell us."

Asa nodded and looked to Dusty. "But first, I think there is something you'd like to say?"

Dusty got to her feet, all eyes on her. "I'm in love with Ty Coltrane."

Everyone looked at her as if waiting for more.

"Of course you are," Shelby said, smiling, as if she'd known it all along.

"He's asked me to marry him," Dusty continued, her gaze shifting to her father. "It's going to be a small wedding. Just family. Tomorrow."

There were sounds of surprise around the table, but Dusty saw her father nod and Shelby start to cry quietly.

"You sure about this?" J.T. asked, looking around the table in confusion. "This is so sudden. You haven't even *dated*."

Dusty smiled. "Someone once told me that when you found your true love, you just knew. You didn't have to kiss a lot of frogs. Or a lot of princes. You just had to know in your heart that this was the right person for you. Ty's my true love." Tears rushed to her eyes as she looked at her father, saw him squeeze the hand of his true love. "I want you to give me away," she said to her father.

His jaw tensed, as if he were fighting to keep his face from showing the emotion she saw in his eyes. "It would be my pleasure," he said, voice cracking.

J.T. let out an expletive. The rest of the family had fallen silent. He looked down the table at his father. "How long do you have?"

"Not long enough."

Epilogue

Rain fell in a light drizzle on the day of Asa McCall's funeral. Dusty stood on the hillside, her husband Ty beside her, his arm around her as she huddled against the cold and wetness and grief.

Across from her stood her brothers Rourke, Cash and Brandon, next to them their wives, their expressions somber as they stared down at their father's casket.

Brandon's eyes filled with tears. Dusty saw Anna clutch his hand tighter. Mason VanHorn held his daughter's hand as he, too, stood in the rain over his once worst enemy's grave. The two had found peace only at the end of Asa's life, a horrible waste that Dusty knew would haunt Mason to his own grave.

Shelby stood between Dusty and her eldest son J.T., his wife Reggie next him.

The pastor cleared this throat. "As anyone standing here knows, Asa McCall wasn't much of a churchgoer." There was a slight nervous titter from the crowd.

"In fact, he didn't hold much patience with a man of the collar." Pastor Grayson smiled. "I remember the first time I met Asa McCall. We got into a discussion about God." He chuckled. "Asa said he had a fine arrangement with God. God tried his patience every day—and Asa tried the Lord's. He said they'd been getting along just fine with that arrangement for years, and he saw no reason to confuse God by acting any different."

A smattering of laughter, then sniffles.

"That strong, sometimes impossible, man is who we are putting to rest here today," the pastor said. "Asa lived life on his terms and took full responsibility for the whole of it. He was a God-fearing man who, like the rest of us, made his share of mistakes." Pastor Grayson looked over at Shelby. "I had the good fortune to speak with Asa before he passed away. He told me of his regrets—the greatest one being not living long enough to see all of his grandchildren."

Dusty blinked back tears. Ty pulled her closer.

"But Asa died knowing that his children and their children would continue the legacy his father had begun so many years ago when he brought the first herd of longhorns to Montana and settled in this valley. That, he told me, was more than he ever could have wanted—to see his lifework continued by his own children and their children."

Pastor Grayson opened the small black Bible in his hands and looked down. "Asa asked me to read this today. It's something he wrote just before he died."

The pastor cleared his voice and began to read, "By the time you hear this, I will be gone from you. Don't mourn my passing. I had a long and fruitful life. Bury me on the hillside with the rest of the McCalls and then get on with your lives. You have a ranch to run and children to make and raise. Don't try to make me into a saint. I was a stubborn jackass. I want my grandchildren to know the man I really was. Maybe it will keep them from making the mistakes I did.

"I ask only one other thing. Take care of your mother. Don't blame her for my asinine behavior so many years ago. Pushing her from my life is my greatest regret, second only to never telling all of you how much I love you, admire you, respect you. You have all made an old man proud."

Tears streamed down Dusty's face as she looked over at her mother and saw the naked grief in her face. Dusty reached out and took her mother's hand. Her mother seemed surprised, then smiled through her tears and squeezed her daughter's hand.

Slowly, Asa McCall's casket was lowered into the ground on the ranch he'd loved. Dusty looked past the old family cemetery to the view of the Big Horn Mountains and McCall land stretching as far as the eye could see. Her father's view for eternity, she thought as she turned her face into Ty's strong shoulder, felt his arms come around her as she said goodbye to her father.

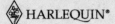

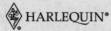

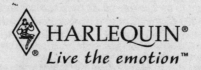

If you enjoyed what you just read,
then we've got an offer you can't resist!

Take 2 bestselling love stories FREE!

Plus get a FREE surprise gift!

Clip this page and mail it to Harlequin Reader Service®

IN U.S.A.	IN CANADA
3010 Walden Ave.	P.O. Box 609
P.O. Box 1867	Fort Erie, Ontario
Buffalo, N.Y. 14240-1867	L2A 5X3

YES! Please send me 2 free Harlequin Intrigue® novels and my free surprise gift. After receiving them, if I don't wish to receive anymore, I can return the shipping statement marked cancel. If I don't cancel, I will receive 4 brand-new novels each month, before they're available in stores! In the U.S.A., bill me at the bargain price of $4.24 plus 25¢ shipping and handling per book and applicable sales tax, if any*. In Canada, bill me at the bargain price of $4.99 plus 25¢ shipping and handling per book and applicable taxes**. That's the complete price and a savings of at least 10% off the cover prices—what a great deal! I understand that accepting the 2 free books and gift places me under no obligation ever to buy any books. I can always return a shipment and cancel at any time. Even if I never buy another book from Harlequin, the 2 free books and gift are mine to keep forever.

181 HDN DZ7N
381 HDN DZ7P

Name	(PLEASE PRINT)	
Address	Apt.#	
City	State/Prov.	Zip/Postal Code

Not valid to current Harlequin Intrigue® subscribers.

Want to try two free books from another series?
Call 1-800-873-8635 or visit www.morefreebooks.com.

* Terms and prices subject to change without notice. Sales tax applicable in N.Y.
** Canadian residents will be charged applicable provincial taxes and GST.
  All orders subject to approval. Offer limited to one per household.
  ® are registered trademarks owned and used by the trademark owner and or its licensee.

INT04R   ©2004 Harlequin Enterprises Limited

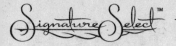

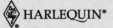